But is it Art?

A Case for Crabbe and Crabbe

Geoffrey Foster

May 2011

Geoffrey Foster was born in London, England in 1933, and his childhood was mostly spent in Kent and the south-eastern suburbs of London, not far from some of the places depicted here.

His father was a London policeman most of his working life, and his mother, when she worked, was a Pitman-trained shorthand typist (like Marjorie and Winnie in this story). He has two sisters, five and thirteen years younger than himself.

He went to public elementary and secondary schools and then to the University of Cambridge, where he studied engineering. Moving to Australia in 1959, he taught for 36 years at the University of Queensland, first Mechanical Engineering and then educational development. He retired early in 1995.

As well as writing, he likes reading, listening to music, solving cryptic crosswords, walking the family beagle, Kafka, and playing tennis with his younger sister, Ynes.

Also by Geoffrey Foster:

Kit and the Beeman   ISBN 978-0-9805310-0-8

Kit the Venturer   ISBN 978-0-9805310-1-5

Vincent the Beeman   ISBN 978-0-9805310-2-2

Beatrice's Birthday   ISBN 978-0-9805310-3-9

Beatrice and Vincent's Welsh Adventures

                            ISBN 978-0-9805310-4-6

Trouble at the Mill: A Case for Crabbe and Crabbe
                            ISBN 978-0-9805310-6-0

This volume   ISBN 978-0-9805310-7-7

Chapter 1

Melpomene and Alexander, the partners in 'Crabbe and Crabbe: Private Investigators' had no trouble finding the DuPlessis Gallery on Kensington High Street, and stood for a few minutes sizing up the shop-front. It certainly looked respectable, even prosperous, and prompted Mel to check her appearance in her reflection in the plate-glass front window, saying, "Mr DuPlessis has probably a different appreciation of fashion from that of our recent clients in industry!"

"Why don't we go in, then, Mel?" said Alex, "You can then see whether or not your imagined picture of our prospective client matches his reality!"

Inside they found a reception area or waiting room, with a long counter of polished mahogany at which sat a elegantly-dressed but bored-looking young man perusing a glossy magazine. As he stood up to greet them, Melpomene glanced at its cover, and was amused to see it was a copy of 'Vogue' at least two years old.

"Good afternoon, Sir and Madam, how can I be of service?" he said. "We have an appointment with Mr DuPlessis, at one o'clock," replied Alex, "we are from the Crabbe and Crabbe agency."

"Oh yes. Please follow me!"

He led them along a short corridor, with the walls almost covered with a selection of oils, watercolours, and drawings. He knocked at a door and, receiving a peremptory "Come!", ushered them into a large office holding several comfortable chairs and settees, but, surprisingly, no desk.

As they entered, Mr DuPlessis stood up, with his hands outstretched, first welcoming Melpomene by clasping her hands between his, and then shaking Alex' firmly.

"I think I can guess which of you is Melpomene, and which Alex!" he said, smiling widely, "But we do, in fact have a female conservator whom we call Alex – I believe her full name must be Alexandra!"

"Can I offer you anything before we get down to business? I often indulge myself with a glass of mineral water from time to time during the working day, but of course we have something a little stronger if you prefer it – or maybe you would like a cup of tea? Anatole will do the honours, I'm sure!"

"Tea would indeed go down very nicely!" said Mel, "Alex will speak for himself!" Alex nodded and smiled, while Anatole said, "I believe we can run to Lapsang Souchong or Earl Grey, whichever you prefer!" They both opted for the former.

"So, with the social niceties over, maybe I should explain my predicament," said DuPlessis, "by the way, since we appear to be on first name terms, please call me Severin – an unusual name which has been traditional in my family since the sixteenth century, they tell me!"

"What happened a week or more ago was that one of my long-term clients or customers – a politician in the North – telephoned me in some agitation and said that the picture I described to your secretary – is Margaret her name? Oh, Marjorie, I'm sorry – that he bought from me recently had been hung in his dining room in a prominent position and had been greatly admired both by him and by most of his guests, until one of them had, rather rudely, gone over to it after dinner one night, peered at it closely, and then said something like, 'You know you've been sold a pup, Arnold!' My client was, of course rather embarrassed and upset about this, but refrained from accusing me of any deceit. My immediate reaction was to say that I was amazed, but that if it did turn out to be not the genuine article, I would of course make it up to him. I should point out that the sum involved is rather large, in the thousands of guineas range!"

"So, what action have you taken so far?" asked Mel, "Did you make any efforts to check on this accusation?"

"Oh, certainly! Someone in my position cannot possibly afford to place a great deal of credence in a snap opinion offered after dinner by someone not a specialist in the field! Next day I telephoned one of my acquaintances living not far from my client and prevailed upon him to go and give a second opinion. I knew I could rely on him to treat the matter with some delicacy."

"Was he able to make any judgment" asked Mel.

"No – because my client, the purchaser, refused to let him inspect the work, saying that he intended to arrange for a completely independent expert, of his own choice, to do so! Fortunately, my acquaintance was not offended, but simply telephoned me to tell me what happened. I have not yet heard from the purchaser – I will give it a day or two before I enquire again. This whole business is getting me quite nervous, which is why I have called on your agency!"

Said Alex, "We are happy that you did so, but I should make a point of which, no doubt, you are already well aware. We are detectives, but neither of us, although we feel we can appreciate a fine work of art, has any expertise in assessing the technical merits of a work, nor of judging its authenticity."

"Do not sell yourselves too short!" said DuPlessis, "It would be possible, in a remarkably short space of time, for either of you to be given the rudiments of a small aspect of the requisite skills. For instance, you will perhaps recognize the term 'craquelure', which refers to the surface texture acquired over time by an oil painting by way of minute cracks. I could, myself, show you enough in a twenty-minute session so that you could tell whether or not this effect is consistent with the age, size and method of mounting of a canvas. I should say that of all the characteristics of an oil painting, the craquelure is least susceptible to undetectable manipulation. But, I am letting my enthusiasm run away with me! We have yet to establish whether or not your agency is willing to accept this assignment, and under what terms!"

Anatole, who had been hovering in the background after bringing a tea-tray and some petits-fours, coughed discreetly at this point and murmured something in DuPlessis' ear.

"Oh yes, of course!" exclaimed DuPlessis, "My assistant has pointed out that I have been rambling on about oil-painting, whereas the work in dispute is an aquarelle! And falsifying or manipulation of that medium is an entirely different matter! Nevertheless, I still contend that either of you would be able to acquire a few skills in that area, given a short period of instruction from me, or perhaps better from Alex Mainwaring, our conservator who I mentioned earlier, who is a water-colourist of note in her own right!"

"We will certainly look forward to such instruction!" said Melpomene, "My feeling, and I believe this is shared by Alex, is that we would gladly undertake to investigate your case!"

"I concur!" said Alex, "The terms can wait until later!"

Chapter 2

"I am pleased and relieved that you have agreed to take this on!" said DuPlessis, "Let me introduce you to Dr Alex Mainwaring and I will try to persuade her to show you a typical aquarelle. Please come with me."

They were led along the corridor, across a large room that evidently formed the main gallery, to a door giving onto a workshop area. Sitting on a stool at a workbench, examining a picture through a large lens on a stand, was a woman, maybe a little older than Mel and Alex, with long black hair tied up in a braid and wearing a smock, originally white but with the front covered in coloured blotches.

"Alex, may I introduce another Alex and Melpomene, who together are the Crabbe detective agency, who are to solve our problem with 'Daphnis and Chloe' for us! I have said that you might explain how an aquarelle is painted, and how it might be susceptible to tampering."

The conservator smiled and stepped forward to shake hands, wiping her own on the back of her smock as she did so, apparently a habitual act, since they seemed to be clean enough.

"You have caught me at a good time, since I am working on a water-colour we have just acquired, rather the worse for wear and needing a little loving care! Let me show you what I was just doing – I have to return to it quickly in any case, because, as you will find out, we workers in the medium are at the mercy of water, which does what it wants to and will not wait for us!"

She got back on the stool, while Mal and Alex stood one each side of her. Looking through the lens, she dipped a small brush into a glass of clean water, then into paint on a saucer, and applied it to the painting. "You will see, if you look closely, that what I am doing is extending this green area, part of the foliage of this tree, so that it covers up an unsightly brown mark – I don't know what it is, maybe even coffee! – but it is certainly a distraction where it is!"

Melpomene said, "Oh yes, I see! Couldn't you just remove it?"

"In fact, I have already done that as much as possible – it was much darker before – but I have to avoid damaging the paper.

7

If you are working on canvas you can do much more drastic repairs, even scraping the paint right back to nothing, but with paper this is not possible. We water-colourists are a much gentler breed!"

"She is right!" said Severin DuPlessis, "I have seen painters in oils scrape away whole areas of their work, and start again from scratch – or just paint over a part of a picture, since oil paints are opaque. It has sometimes been found, by people restoring old works, that there is a completely different figure underneath – maybe that gentleman lost favour at court or died or something of the sort!"

"What I'm wondering," said Alex Crabbe, "is why your client's interfering dinner guest was so convinced that the painting was questionable. Has your client given you any idea of this?"

"No, and as far as I can see, I shall have to visit him and have him explain the basis for that provocative accusation! And it will have to be done in front of the painting itself, of course. Would either or both of you be willing to accompany me to his home and find out as much of this dismal story as we can? I can play down the fact that you are detectives, if you like, just introduce you as someone with a general interest in acquiring watercolours of that era."

"Certainly we will, won't we – maybe just Melpomene by herself – so as not to appear over-anxious. Please go ahead and make the arrangements, Severin. You said your client is in the North, what town would that be? And perhaps you would be willing to tell us his name – you may rest assured that any enquiries we make will be in complete confidence, and done with the utmost discretion. If you also know, or can find out, the identity of the accuser, this might be valuable, too. I imagine that there is a degree of urgency here – the longer this is left, the wider the pool of rumours will spread."

"Yes, of course!" said Severin, "As I think I have mentioned before, our whole business relies on good will and unsullied reputations! I will let you know as soon as we have worked something out and telephone you at your office, or your secretary – she seems to be an exceptionally competent person! The town in question is Northampton, a mainly manufacturing city. My client owns a large boot and shoe factory there. I will send all those details to your office as soon as possible."

They bid Severin and Alex Mainwaring a cordial goodbye, and left the premises to go back to their Alvis, parked in a side-street. After the usual amiable argument about who would drive, Melpomene won and took the wheel, and they were soon back at their office in Finsbury Park. Marjorie greeted them as they walked in, saying "Cups of tea, of course? No jam tarts today, I'm afraid, Mrs Jenkins sold out before I could get down there – but we've got some of those chocolate biscuits you both like, so they will have to do!"

"Any calls?" asked Mel.

"Only one, from your friend Detective-Sergeant Manley at Mile End Road – he wanted to let you know that Wilfred Hutchinson was picked up by the Huddersfield police, for speeding in the centre of the city and striking out at the officer who stopped him! So he is now under arrest, and perhaps you can close your case file on him soon!"

Marjorie went on, "And no mail today – except bills of course! I'll go and make the tea."

They sat and enjoyed their tea and biscuits, then Alex said, "I wonder what culinary delights Mrs Mountain has prepared for us tonight. Should we get a couple of bottles of red on the way home? As far as I can recall we've almost completely exhausted our cellar."

"Good thinking, Alex! Will you come and have dinner with us at the flat, Marjorie, to celebrate us picking up a new case, since we had substantial assistance from you?"

"Not tonight, thanks, Mel, but good of you to ask! I have to get home to my Mum – she is starting to feel Winter coming on, even though it's a while yet. I'll see you in the morning, will I?"

"Oh yes," replied Mel, "we haven't made any arrangements for our new job yet, but I think we might go to the Victoria and Albert soon, to get a bit more of a feel about watercolours."

"And I was thinking of the Wallace Collection, too," said Alex, "apparently they specialize in seventeenth and eighteenth century works. But it's a private collection so I don't know how accessible it is. I'll make some enquiries."

Mel said, "Why don't we ask Alex Mainwaring – she'd be able to point us in the right direction, surely. When Severin phones, I'll ask if I may speak to her too. I rather like her!"

Chapter 3

Over breakfast, Alex said that he had just recalled reading, a couple of years ago, an article about a big scandal involving fake Old Masters, "I've been racking my brains trying to remember where it was I read about it. The impression that has stayed with me is that a half-successful painter had turned to counterfeiting as a more profitable endeavour!"

"That rings a bell with me, too!" said Melpomene, "Was it in one of the illustrated magazines? There were pictures, too, as I recall. Perhaps it was in 'The Illustrated London News', that's a weekly that would be likely to pick up such a story."

"Let's ask Marjorie whether they keep back numbers at the local library, or whether we might need to go somewhere like a University library," said Alex, "I'll telephone University College library later this morning. I could ask if anyone there recalled such an article, too."

"Now you've set my mind working!" said Melpomene, "Where have we recently seen a young man in the art world who has time to read magazines? Rhetorical question – it was Anatole, at the DuPlessis Gallery! I trust you've got the number in your little book, Alex! I'll try him straight away."

Anatole answered DuPlessis' phone – apparently he acted as a secretary as well as receptionist and tea-maker!

"DuPlessis Gallery – Anatole Simpson speaking – how can I help you?"

"Melpomene Crabbe here – my partner and I were there yesterday afternoon. You may remember me – I am the shorter of the two, quite slight and pretty, with blonde curls! We are looking for an article about an art forgery that might have been in 'The Illustrated London News' or some similar publication, a couple of years ago. Ring any bells for you, Anatole?"

"Of course I remember you, Melpomene – you were wearing a little number in sage-green jersey – by Chanel, if I'm any judge! But I can't put my finger on the article you're after – leave it with me – we have back numbers of that magazine going back several years – it often runs art-related stories. Do we have your telephone number?"

"You have our office number, Anatole, but I'll give you our home number – Finsbury 1692 – please make sure that Severin gets it too – but perhaps you do all his telephoning, as well? Look forward to hearing from you – we shall be here in the flat for at least another hour. Is Alex Mainwaring in at the moment? I wouldn't mind a word with her if she's there."

"No, she hasn't come in yet. I think she was here until all hours last night, working on that aquarelle. She left me a note to say she was eventually satisfied with it but would take another look today, when it is thoroughly dry. Can I get her to ring when she arrives?"

"No thanks, Anatole, we are going to be buzzing about later – but still let us know if you locate that article in the next hour, and we can go and look it up at a library somewhere."

Melpomene put the telephone down and felt to see whether the teapot was still warm. "I'll make another pot – all that telephoning has left me parched. Could you drink a third cup, Alex? And then why don't we go to the office? Otherwise I'll be talking to Marjorie on the telephone all over again!"

They parked the Alvis round the corner from the office and climbed the stairs. Marjorie greeted them cheerily, "You've beaten the postman this morning, but you just got a couple of calls. One was from Superintendent Wilkinson, at Woodhampton – nothing new, he said, just keeping in touch – I think he really enjoyed your last case, and he is feeling a little too tranquil and rural now!"

"Good old David!" said Alex, "I hardly think our new case will call for his services – but who knows? What was the other call?"

"That was from someone whose name I didn't recognize – a gentleman with a foreign accent – not French, I think, more like German or Dutch – he left his name and number and would like you to call back. Let me see – here we are – Jens-Olle Pedersen – he spelt it for me."

"That name sounds more Scandinavian than German," said Mel, "did he say what he wanted?"

"No, he said it was highly confidential and he would rather speak with Melpomene, because he had been given her name by an associate. Would you like me to call his number?"

"Certainly, Marjorie, I'm somewhat intrigued! I'll take it in the back office as it's so confidential!"

The voice on the phone was indeed accented, but the caller's language was otherwise meticulous.

"You may be puzzled that I asked for you, Frøken Crabbe," he said, "but I was given your name by a colleague in the French Sûreté, Commissaire Principal Hugo Palance. We are both members of an international committee of police officers dealing with smuggling and other illegal cross-border transactions. I hold the position of Assistant Commissioner of the Copenhagen Division, and am the guest at the moment of the equivalent section of Scotland Yard, who I am working with in an attempt to get to grips with an international gang of art thieves. Hugo Palance, I should tell you, was greatly impressed with your agency's work in bringing the members of the Pilkington gang to book."

"But, Mr Pedersen," said Melpomene, "how can a small set-up like ours possibly add any value to your extensive organisation of highly-experienced expert officers?"

"To explain how it can, I shall tell you something extremely sensitive and confidential, but I will only do this face-to-face and on the condition you and your partner sign a document which will bind you to secrecy under the weight of the most severe penalties. If you are willing to proceed, nevertheless, I will come to your office at a day and hour that you nominate and explain fully."

Alex, who had been listening on the second earpiece, nodded, so Melpomene said, "Very well, Mr Pedersen, how about this afternoon at 4.30? I gather you are in London and can find us!"

"Very good!" said Pederson, "I look forward to meeting you and your partner – 4.30 it shall be!"

When she had rung off, Melpomene moved to Alex and hugged him. "This certainly calls for a cup of tea!" then she called. "Marjorie, tea and jam tarts – I hope you did not fail in that respect two days running!"

"Of course not, Mel! I was on Mrs Jenkins' doorstep as she opened up this morning, and she had a box of tarts ready waiting for us! I'll go and make a pot of Lapsang Souchong and one of Earl Grey immediately!"

Chapter 4

No sooner had they started on the tea and jam tarts when the doorbell rang. Marjorie jumped up, dabbing jam from the corners of her mouth, and went to answer the door. Then she brought in Anatole, carrying a portfolio and grinning somewhat apologetically.

"Another cup and plate, please, Marjorie!" said Alex, showing Anatole to a chair, "I hope you like Lapsang Souchong! What have you brought for us?"

"I'm sorry to intrude like this," said the young man, "Severin was anxious for you to get the information he promised, so he asked me to drive here, instead of entrusting it to the post office, and, while he was putting it together, I managed to find that issue of the 'Illustrated London News' with the article about the art forger. Here it is! Now I've reread it, I can remember almost all the details."

"Let me see," said Melpomene, "I seem to recall that the forger had a foreign name – what was it, now? Backer? Wicker?"

"Here it is!" said Anatole, "Otto Wacker was his name – a German art dealer who commissioned forgeries, or painted them himself – it is still unclear – of a large number of Van Goghs, causing great confusion. Some of the purchasers insisted they were genuine, even after evidence to the contrary was shown them. The matter is still being pursued by the authorities here and on the continent, and there is no doubt that this man will be brought to justice before many years are out!"

Alex intervened in this lively discussion, "I know it was I who brought this up originally, but we shouldn't let it run away with us! We are not dealing with a forgery at the moment – at least, I don't believe so. What we have is merely an accusation that a painting sold to this man by the DuPlessis Gallery is not what it was claimed to be. If we get obsessed with forgery it will distract us from our duty as investigators – which is to determine facts! Am I right?"

The others agreed. "Now," Alex continued, "Anatole, will you show us what Severin has sent us, please?"

"First," said Anatole, "here are the details about the customer who bought the work. I will summarize them – you can read the notes thoroughly later. His name is Arnold Henderson, he is the owner of Henderson & Frears' boot and shoe factory – Frears died a decade ago – and he is also the MP for Northampton Central, for the Liberals – a lost cause, I fear, given their pathetic results at the last election. He is seriously rich, but in my judgment he feels that he is still having to work hard to take his rightful place in society and has not got there yet. So his art collection, such as it is, is seen by him as an important status symbol."

"What sort of a man is he, apart from all that?" asked Melpomene.

"He is not unpleasant, as Severin tells it, rather jovial in fact – I have never met the man, but he is always polite to me on the telephone, even when he is complaining. And the other person in question, that self-appointed arbiter of true and false in art, is a merchant of the city, a Mr Luke Postlethwaite, who owns three general groceries, a hardware store and a supplier of building materials. As far as I know, he possesses no works of art himself. I have not met him either, but he was described to Severin by Mr Henderson as 'more noisy than effective – wants to be noticed!'."

"What are the other documents that Severin has sent?" asked Alex.

"A copy of the bill of sale for 'Daphnis and Chloe with Putti' on which it is described as '18C, *English School, unsigned and otherwise unattributed, aquarelle with some opaque watercolour, bond paper mounted on board, 35 by 27 inches, slight foxing on lower edge under frame, modern gilt frame.*' I have also brought a second copy of the sale catalogue – I believe you already have one – and a statement of provenance which gives the name of the dealer from whom Severin obtained the work, together with a list of acknowledged former owners – incomplete, of course, as they often are. Lastly, there are copies of three letters, the correspondence between Mr Henderson and Mr DuPlessis."

"While I think of it, Anatole," said Alex, "what does 'putti' mean?"

"They are figures of naked male babies – a common motif of early artistic periods – a lay person would call them 'cupids'."

"Oh yes, I see what you mean!" said Alex, looking at the catalogue. "While I have it in mind, how are the illustrations for catalogues produced? I understand that they must be rather imprecise – and maybe the colours are not particularly true – so would be only a rough guide for a purchaser, is that the case?"

"That is so," replied Anatole, "no serious buyer would accept such a picture without viewing the original. For our catalogues, we rely on the services of a professional photographer in Chelsea who brings his equipment and sets it up in our main gallery. He uses a full-plate camera so as to get the most accurate result, then he takes the plates to the printing house who design and print our catalogues, and they reduce the pictures to a suitable size. As you say, there is an inevitable loss in colour and fine detail."

"Thank you, Anatole," said Alex, "this has all been very helpful! I assume that if we have any questions we can telephone you? And I know that Melpomene wants to speak to Alex Mainwaring, when she gets a chance. I'm afraid we will have to bid you farewell for the present – we are shortly expecting a visit from a client on an entirely different case. Look forward to seeing you again!"

He and Mel shook his hand and showed him to the street door.

"Now," said Melpomene, "I'm wondering how we shall find Jens-Olle Pedersen and what he has in mind for us. Do you think we can run two cases simultaneously, Alex?"

"I don't see why not," Alex replied, "one of the benefits of being a partnership is that we can work independently from time to time, as you did so effectively in the Pilkington affair! Maybe, come to think of it, it would be a good idea for you to have a pistol of your own – maybe a dear little Beretta that you can keep in your handbag!"

They both chuckled at this, but Alex could see that it had started a chain of thought for Mel, and she made a couple of abstracted motions as though she was aiming a gun.

Then there was another ring of the doorbell, and Marjorie jumped up to answer it. She brought Mr Pedersen into the main office, introduced Mel and Alex to him and retired to the front desk, shutting the door behind her.

Jens-Olle was tall, fresh-faced and blond, reminding Mel of a Swedish ski instructor that she had been attracted to on a University vacation trip, but then told herself that there was probably not much skiing in Denmark.

Chapter 5

Jens-Olle Pedersen greeted them affably enough, but it was apparent that he was suffering some sort of strain, even sighing as he accepted a cup of tea and sank into a chair.

"I told you that there were sensitive issues in the work that I am engaged in. I also said that it involved collaboration between several police services, in Denmark, France and Great Britain, among others. Our opponents also work in a collaborative way, with links between gangs and individual criminals in each of those countries and also, some of us believe, the USA, especially since Prohibition. We have not contacted any American police, nor the FBI, and we have good reasons for this, as I shall explain later on."

He took a sip of tea and sighed again, "I am deeply grateful that the Asiatic organizations, such as the Chinese Tongs, the Japanese Yakuza and their equivalents in Malaya, Burma and Borneo have so far not interested themselves in the European scene – whereas they are rampant in the USA, Canada and Latin America. The European opium trade has been relatively quiet lately."

"But drugs are but one aspect of international crime, which impinges on our work but does not dominate it. We have set our sights differently – admittedly for pragmatic reasons – and are concentrating on such issues as the smuggling of arms and other highly valuable commodities, including art of various kinds, antiquities, jewellery and items of vertu."

Alex asked, "I am getting a sense that those interested in these commodities are a cut above your ordinary villain – is this so?"

"Alex, I am impressed, you have hit the nail on the head!" Jens-Olle sat up straight, "And therein lies our predicament. Many of these people occupy positions of high social and political prominence and have wide influence. And the worst of it is that, in my belief and that of some of my close associates, they have infiltrated the ranks of our organization and because of their general high intelligence they are able to conceal themselves effectively."

"So this is where we come in!" exclaimed Melpomene.

"You are right again!", said Jens-Olle, "And this is a good moment for me to ask you to sign non-disclosure agreements! If you are going to participate effectively, I and some of my close colleagues, such as Hugo Palance, will be entrusting you with information that must be strictly quarantined, and we need to safeguard ourselves. Trust based on respect and 'gentlemen's agreements' will not serve here, I fear. We need, and I regret this, to have legally-enforceable instruments. I have had some copies prepared – please read them through, and if you have any misgivings, now is the time to raise them. I know that Alex is a lawyer, so the language will be familiar to him – if, Melpomene, you require any clarification, he and I between us should be able to provide it. When the time comes to sign, perhaps your secretary would be so good as to act as a second witness."

"This process calls for further cups of tea!" said Melpomene, "Unless, Jens-Olle, you would prefer coffee? Yes? I will ask Marjorie to make it. When the business is finished, we might indulge in something a little stronger!"

The next hour was spent in careful perusal of the documents, and, indeed, the occasional wording or point of law needed elucidating. Eventually, all were satisfied, and Alex and Melpomene each signed two copies, one to keep in the office safe and one for Jens-Olle to take.

"Now," said Jens-Olle, "I shall give you one or two hints of the reasons for my paranoia about security. I shall start with the first incident that started our worries off. This was at a meeting I had convened in Copenhagen – we try to rotate our activities among our members – when Hugo Palance was relating the story of an encounter – or rather a non-encounter – of one of his officers in the docks at Marseilles with a group of smugglers. It was not known at the time what goods were involved, but there had been a tip-off by a customs agent who thought he recognised one of the men. He had been unwilling to confront him, as there was no evidence at the time of any attempt at illicit imports, and there had been a considerable – what is your English word? – hoo-hah a few months earlier, when this businessman had been intercepted carrying a suitcase with a false bottom. He had objected vigorously to being questioned, insisting the case be searched, whereupon nothing of an illicit nature was found. He claimed that the so-called false bottom was merely a compartment he used to carry his dress shirts without them getting creased, and threatened to make an official complaint."

"Sounds a bit like setting up a smokescreen!" said Melpomene.

Jens-Olle smiled and nodded and returned to the incident he had been describing, "On spotting this man this time, the customs agent kept well away and telephoned Hugo's special squad, by way of a number known to the customs staff as a contact for use in similar situations. The senior man in the squad on duty at the docks, dressed in civilian clothes, then strolled casually past the suspect without appearing to pay him any attention. To his surprise, he heard his name mentioned, and turned to see the suspect pointing him out to a companion!"

Jens-Ole paused, and then said, "This has turned out to be a long story, so I will get straight to the point! There was no way that the squad leader's name could have been learned by the smuggler other than through internal channels – the customs people had the telephone number, that was all. Hugo concluded that there was an informer among us. There are other similar stories I could tell, but that will suffice for now. We must assume that there are those in our organization that are indiscreet at the least, and criminal at the worst!"

Then Melpomene thanked him, saying, "I am beginning to see what the role of Crabbe and Crabbe might be!" and suggested that they seal their contract at a restaurant, "All this thinking has given me an appetite!" she declared, "Will you join us, Jens-Olle?"

"Forgive me, Melpomene, if I do not," he replied, "I spent all day yesterday travelling, and I had meetings all morning here at Scotland Yard, so I had better go straight to my hotel, have a quick meal and go to bed, if the efficient Marjorie would be so kind as to fetch me a taxi!"

"No, no!", said Alex, "We shall drive you, if you don't mind an open car. Mel can take the dicky seat and then we will drop you at your hotel and go on to our flat, where our redoubtable Mrs Mountain will prepare one of her impromptu feasts for us!"

And so, in less than an hour, they were sitting down to what Mrs Mountain referred to as "toad in the 'ole with trimmins", a surprisingly delicious compound of sausages, batter and sautéed vegetables.

Chapter 6

As they were getting ready to go to bed, Melpomene said, "My mind has been so occupied with Jens-Olle's concerns, that I've forgotten all about Severin DuPlessis. We should telephone him first thing in the morning and work out what we should do about visiting Northampton. Maybe we'll get a chance of talking to Alex Mainwaring a bit more – I'm still wondering just what it could have been that Luke Postlethwaite spotted to make him suspicious – it couldn't have been very subtle if a shopkeeper could spot it!"

"Now, now, Mel!" said Alex, "Let us not show our condescension – for all we know he could be a highly cultured gentleman! Nevertheless, you may have a point – have your cup of chocolate and try not to worry about it all night!"

As she had planned, Melpomene telephoned the DuPlessis Gallery straight after breakfast and was slightly surprised when, instead of Anatole, Severin answered.

"I was wondering about what arrangements we should make to visit Arnold Henderson to view the disputed picture," she said, "Alex and I think that only one of us should go, so as not to be overpowering. Maybe I should be the one – what do you think, Severin?"

"Good morning, Melpomene – how I like pronouncing your name! – one of the problems is catching him at home. The House is sitting until this weekend, and he spends quite a bit of time at his factory too, so he is only at home in small spells. But, come to think of it, he may agree to us inspecting the picture without him – he will probably want his wife, or a trusted servant or friend to stand by while we do it, but this is no problem to us, is it? And a further thought – perhaps I should stand aside myself, since I have the most intense interest in the outcome."

Melpomene thought a little and then replied, "How about this as a proposition, Severin – the delegation should consist of two people only, myself as an independent investigator, accompanied by Alex Mainwaring to represent the gallery and contribute her expertise in watercolour techniques. Does that sound feasible to you?"

"Very good, Melpomene – and the fact that you are both women will make the exercise even less threatening to Henderson – unless, of course, he is a misogynist! Would you like me to try to make the arrangements, or will you?"

"Why not leave them to Anatole?" said Mel, "He seems very good at this sort of thing."

"So it shall be!" announced Severin in a satisfied tone, "I'm feeling very positive about all this!"

Mel reported all this to Alex, who agreed that it was a sound plan. "And now," he said, "while you were talking to Severin, I was thinking about this Luke Postlethwaite, and wondering about his motives in denigrating the picture, ranging from the childish one of simply scoring points off an acquaintance, all the way to hatching a plot to devalue the work so he could step in and acquire it for a bargain price!"

"I see what you mean, Alex, but if he bought it in such an underhand manner, he could hardly hang it at home, could he? He would have to be a complete narcissist, like I took Pilkington to be, wouldn't he?"

"I get your point, Mel," said Alex, "but that idea makes me fantasise further – perhaps he is doing all this on behalf of a prospective buyer in the shadows! You know, I think I will ask Jens-Olle if Postlethwaite's name has ever come up in his investigations. We know what hotel he is staying at, let's try telephoning!"

"Yes," agreed Mel, "but let's go to the office to do all this – Marjorie could help in the arrangements."

At the office, Marjorie greeted them with the most important item first. "Everything is fine – the jam tart situation is under control, and by the way, the Danish gentleman called to tell you he would be at the Yard this afternoon, but will be at the hotel until about noon – I wrote down his direct telephone number."

"Oh, good," said Melpomene, "Can you ring him now, please?"

When Jens-Olle spoke to her, he said that he had informed those of his colleagues that he could trust about the arrangements made the day before, and that they were very pleased with them. He went on, "Did you have anything you wanted to ask me now? They are sending a car to take me to New Scotland Yard quite soon."

Mel told him about Postlethwaite and Alex' theory on the reason he made disparaging remarks about Henderson's picture and asked him if the name meant anything to him.

"Please spell it for me, Melpomene, some of your English names are a bit difficult for a Dane. Right – I would have pronounced it 'Post-lee-ther-waite' – it does not ring any immediate bells with me, but I will contact those at our bureaux in each country who keep our records and let you know if any have heard of him. Good – we have already started to collaborate!"

While they were enjoying their next round of cups of tea and jam tarts for the morning, Anatole rang, saying, "I got in touch with Mrs Henderson – as you thought, her husband was away – and put our proposition to her. She saw no problems with it, but said she would check with him later – apparently he makes a point of telephoning home every day when he is in Westminster – and would let us know if and when you and our Alex could make a visit. I had spoken with Alex first, and she said she was quite keen on the idea – it gets her out of the workroom and makes a different use of her expertise."

"You must have been out when I rang before, Anatole," said Mel, "thanks for calling back so promptly."

"Yes, Severin has a weekly chore for me – I have to buy him two pairs of white cotton socks every week in a particular Bond Street store. I don't mind, I usually fit in some of my own shopping – this morning I found a gorgeous mauve voile shirt that will complement my leisure wear admirably!"

"That sounds lovely!" said Mel, "So will you let us know when the arrangements for the Northampton trip have been fixed? Tell Alex that we shall be driving there in our Alvis, so she should wear warmish clothes or a dust-coat and a hat that will not blow off – I either wear a cap on backwards or a cloche!"

Once Anatole had rung off, Melpomene briefed Alex, saying, "I am more and more impressed with Anatole – it appears he can turn his hand without demur to a variety of tasks!"

"We should bear him in mind for our other case," said Alex, "someone with his comprehensive knowledge of the art trade could be very useful to us!"

"And I feel he could be very discreet if required!" said Melpomene.

Chapter 7

The rest of the afternoon was spent partly in general discussion but mainly in relaxation. As Melpomene declared, "All work and no play makes Jack a dull boy!", so she embarked on The Times crossword, while Alex looked through the cinema pages in The Trumpet.

"I say, Mel!" he exclaimed after a while, "They are showing this new talking picture 'The Jazz Singer' at the Piccadilly Theatre – should we try and get in? Apparently the queues were horrific when it opened a few days ago, but it says they're settling down now. There are performances at 6.30 and 8.30!"

"You're on!" said Mel, "I'll ring Mrs M and see if she can manage an early dinner for us, then we can see if we can catch the second show. They say that it is quite an experience to actually hear Al Jolson sing as well as seeing him act! I bet that in three or four years' time the silent movie will be a thing of the past!"

They told Marjorie of their plans and said that, if Jens-Olle called before she left, she should ask him to ring them at home, otherwise they would get back to him in the morning.

All went to plan, and they drove back home after the show full of what they had seen and discussing it enthusiastically. There was a note waiting for them from Caroline, the housemaid, who had gone to bed by then, noting a call from Jens-Olle, who had said that there was nothing on record at any of the bureaux about anyone called Postlethwaite. "So that's a dead end!" said Alex, "It was only ever a faint possibility. Never mind, press on regardless! We'll telephone Anatole in the morning and see if there's anything happening about your trip to Northampton."

After breakfast, they drove to the office, and Melpomene was about to make the call to Anatole when the doorbell rang and Marjorie showed in not only Anatole, but Alex Mainwaring too!

"Mrs Henderson rang and said we could go up there this afternoon," said she, "so I thought it would save time if I came straight round. I don't know how much room you have in your sports car, but I've brought everything I thought might be useful. Anatole says he can take it back to the gallery if I don't take it – we came in Severin's Rolls which he doesn't usually let Anatole use for errands, so I feel honoured!"

"Should we telephone Mrs Henderson to confirm?" asked Melpomene. "No, I took it upon myself to accept! By the way, we are going to get very mixed up between two people called Alex, so why don't you call me Sandy? My Mum has called me that since I was little and couldn't pronounce Alexandra – she doesn't like Alex for some reason, though everybody else does!"

"What did you bring, then, Sandy!" asked Alex, "You'd be surprised how much we can fit in the dicky seat of the Alvis."

"Well, I hardly ever go anywhere without a quarto block of Whatman paper and some brushes and paints and rags and a medicine-bottle of water, in case I see anything that takes my fancy, and some years ago I made a colour chart annotated with the names of various pigments. All this goes in a rather battered attaché case. Finally I have a great big hand lens that I picked up at a sale years ago – I always tell people it belonged to Sherlock Holmes!"

"That's it!" exclaimed Alex, "I've had a sneaking feeling for years that every professional detective ought to possess a hand lens!"

"And what about my clothes, Mel?" said Sandy, "I thought I should wear a presentable frock, in case Mrs Henderson takes notice of such things, but I also brought my ulster – I don't have a dust-coat – and of course I have a cloche hat. Will I be alright in your two-seater with that?"

"If it were winter, you would need more, but that sounds perfect to me," said Melpomene, "well, what are we waiting for, why don't we just pack up and go? When are we expected, Sandy?"

"She just said, 'this afternoon' so we have some latitude."

"And we can stop for lunch *en route* – we should be able to make Northampton in not more than two hours, wouldn't you say, Alex – my Alex, that is, not Sandy – and do we have an exact address for the Hendersons with us? And their telephone number, just in case?"

Anatole came down to have a look at the Alvis – he had missed seeing it when the pair were at the gallery – and drooled over it a little, saying, "I have to drive my Morris Eight most of the time – it's a good little car, but not glamorous!"

At about half past two, Melpomene pulled the car up outside the iron gates of a prosperous-looking house on the outskirts of the city. Sandy got out and pushed a button on one of the gate-posts, whereupon a man, looking like a gardener, came and asked through the gate what their business was. He was satisfied with the reply and pulled open the gates enough for the car to be driven through, saying, "Park your car anywhere on the drive, Miss, the Master is the only one here with a car, and he and his chauffeur are up in London till the weekend. Just ring the doorbell and someone will answer."

Sandy took him at his word as he vanished round the side of the house, pausing only to fetch her equipment from the dicky-seat, and they had to wait only a minute or two after she rang before the door was opened and a maid, dressed neatly in black with a white pinafore and collar, invited them in, saying, "Would you ladies be Mrs Crabbe and Miss Mainwaring?"

They were taken straight to the dining room, where a plump lady with grey hair in a bun, dressed plainly in a blue woollen dress, was standing and smiling. She came forward and took their hands in turn, saying, "I thought we should get straight down to business, then we can chat over refreshments later. I am Mildred Henderson. I can guess which of you is the artist – forgive me mentioning it, my dear, but your fingers give you away, even though the staining is faint! In my time I too have been a water-colourist, although strictly an amateur!"

She took them to stand in front of the disputed picture and said, "First of all, I can assure you that I myself have absolutely no doubt that this 'Daphnis and Chloe' is what Mr DuPlessis claimed it to be, a genuine example of the work of the English water-colour school. But my dear husband has been persuaded otherwise for some dark reason, and will take no notice of my opinion. He is quick to come to decisions – I suppose that is one of the marks of a successful businessman, although I feel that it may not be as useful a characteristic for a politician!"

Turning to Sandy, she said, "Please examine it thoroughly – use your magnifying glass if you like – and see whether you can find anything that would challenge my opinion. You will understand that this is for my satisfaction only. Whatever you say, Arnold will claim you are just supporting your employer!"

Chapter 8

Mrs Henderson and Melpomene sat together watching at one side of the room, while Sandy peered, first from a distance and then closely, at the picture, and looked at various parts of it with her lens. She even took out her colour chart, selected various parts of the scene and made a note of the pigments that came closest. After almost an hour, she stood back, turned to the others and said, "I'll be blowed if I can find anything wrong with this at all!"

"As I thought!" said Mildred Henderson, "Now let us go and have some tea and cake, and I will try to resolve your perplexity about the reason that I set up this whole charade."

She took them into an adjacent sitting-room, rang a bell, and the maid brought in a tea-tray. "Only Ceylon, I'm afraid," Mildred said, "my husband's small-c conservatism pervades the whole establishment, I fear!"

"Now I must at last explain myself. You have, I'm afraid, have both been brought here to some degree under false pretences, while I took advantage of the approach you had made to us. The reason I asked you to come is wider than what Severin DuPlessis had in mind – to validate the picture and exonerate him of dishonesty – but goes much further, to investigate the accuser, his motives and his associates. I suspect, as I believe you might too, that there are dark undercurrents here, that Mr Luke Postlethwaite was put up to denouncing the picture for a reason that has yet to emerge clearly, but is manifestly malicious and quite possibly even criminal. We need to find the underlying reason and try to unmask the instigator or instigators. It is you, Melpomene, and your partner, as professional detectives, who will undertake the major part of this enquiry. Do you accept my apologies?"

They both smiled and nodded.

"Now," said Mildred, "I will relate to you what I believe are some rather important matters that arose after the famous dinner-party. We follow here the rather dated custom that, at the end of a meal, the ladies withdraw – to this sitting-room – I refuse to call it the drawing-room – while the men stay at table enjoying liqueurs or port, cigars – and lewd conversation, I suspect! After an hour or so, I recalled that Arnold had ordered the car for early the next morning, as he had to attend a Liberal Party meeting in Westminster. I thought I had better remind him, so I ventured back into the dining-room and gave him that message – for which he thanked me sincerely. I left, but not before noticing a group at the end of the table who were engaged in some deep discussion – they had glanced rather shiftily at me as I spoke to Arnold, so I made a point of noting who they were, and later wrote a note to myself lest I forgot. I will read the list to you now."

Melpomene took out her own note-pad and prepared to take notes.

Mildred referred to her piece of paper, "Luke Postlethwaite – of course – then a Mr Barker – I don't know his first name, the others called him 'Fido' which I took to be a play on his surname – they behave like schoolboys, these businessmen! Then there was Malcolm Perkins – I am quite friendly with his wife, Naomi – he owns a cartage business around the county. Next, someone who has known Arnold for several years, an accountant called Patrick Benson, and the fifth member of the group was William Satterfield, who I think is in some sort of wholesale trade. As I said, they had their heads together in deep conversation as I entered, paused while I spoke to Arnold, and then seemed to resume as I left. They were grouped together at the end of the table, talking completely separately from the other guests. Do you, Melpomene, like me, suspect that they were up to something?"

Melpomene thought a moment and then said, "I think you have something there, Mildred. At the London School of Economics I studied Social Anthropology, which amongst other topics concerns itself with the behaviour of groups and their members. What you have described fits closely what might be expected from a cohesive group sharing a common goal. It certainly looks as though we have some sort of clique here!"

"I'm so glad you agree with me, Melpomene! I have been stewing over this since that dinner party, so it's good to get it off my chest. I have said nothing to anyone else about my ideas, least of all Arnold! Do you think you and Alex will be able to make use of any of it?"

"Of that I am confident!" replied Melpomene, "We should be able at the very least to settle the dispute between your husband and the DuPlessis Gallery, and it is possible that this will lead us further. We shall see!"

Mildred Henderson pressed Mel and Sandy to stay for dinner, but they made their excuses and got back into the Alvis, waving cheerily to Mildred as they drove away.

"What time is it, Sandy?" asked Melpomene, "Although we refused Mildred's hospitality I have the feeling that we shall need sustenance on the way back to London!"

Consequently, halfway through their journey, the two made a foray into a highway café largely frequented by lorry drivers, where they eagerly consumed bacon sandwiches washed down with mugs of strong sweet tea.

They arrived back at the flat, however, with plenty of appetite for one of Mrs M's dinners of Osso Bucco, over which they related their experience to Alex, who said, "We must tell Jens-Olle those names as soon as possible – he may not have found Postlethwaite alone, but along with Barker, Perkins, Benson and Satterfield in combination it might mean something to one or other of his bureaux. I will try his hotel number – I forget when he said he would be returning to Copenhagen."

A blank was drawn at the hotel, so Alex tried Scotland Yard, asking for Assistant Commissioner Pedersen of the International Task Force. The person who answered merely said that he was unable to help. So Alex said to the others, "All we can do, I'm afraid, is wait for Jens-Olle to contact us, either here or at the office. He knows both numbers."

As they sat around after the meal, Sandy said, "It looks as though we have made little progress on our task of vindicating Severin and the gallery. I suppose we shall just have to wait around until your Danish friend can make some headway with his enquiries. I must confess, I am rather disappointed!"

"But," said Melpomene, "you forget that we can follow up these leads ourselves – Alex and I are professional detectives, you know! First thing in the morning, we shall start tracking down this evil quintet, or my name and that of Alex are not worthy to be associated with those of Auguste Dupin, Sherlock Holmes, Sergeant Cuff or even Sexton Blake!"

"Changing the subject," said Alex, "Sandy, do you want me to drive you home?" "Oh, yes please!" she replied, "I am nearly nodding off already!"

Chapter 9

Soon after they reached the office the next day, the telephone rang and Melpomene said, "I hope this is Jens-Olle! I'm getting quite anxious being out of touch for so long – I keep wondering whether his case will all fall through – and I was getting really interested!"

But it was not Pedersen – when Marjorie picked up the receiver, she announced that it was Severin DuPlessis on the line. She passed the telephone to Mel, who said, "Good morning, Severin, not much of an outcome yet, I'm afraid. We visited Mrs Henderson yesterday afternoon – have you met her? I was most impressed with her intelligence. Perhaps your Alex – who we are calling Sandy, by the way, to avoid confusion with our Alex – has told you all about our visit already. Were you calling us about this, or something else?"

"Hello, Melpomene – yes, Alex has filled me in and tells me you intend to investigate some of Postlethwaite's associates, too, which could be worthwhile. Actually I called on a different matter – I shall be going to a major estate sale in Berkshire tomorrow and I wondered whether you and your husband would like to come. It might give you some insights into the field of art dealing that could be useful in your enquiries."

"Yes, Severin, thank you for the thought!" said Mel, "I would love to come, and Alex, too – he has been listening on the other earpiece and he is nodding enthusiastically!"

"Very good, Mel and Alex!" said Severin, "It is the sort of sale that occasionally happens when there is a family dispute among heirs. The late Lord Sedgwick changed his will several times and there has been litigation since he passed on, with the outcome that everything in the manor house is to be sold at auction – and then there will be a renewed dispute about the proceeds, I suppose. Fortunately that is none of my concern! I have my eye on the pictures, of course. According to the catalogue for the sale – which gives the appearance of having been thrown together in somewhat of a hurry – there are several works that I would be interested in bidding for. There are also some articles of *vertu* I might consider – but I am certainly not interested in the furniture or carpets."

"We could keep our own eyes open for bargains!" Said Mel, "We might one day move into somewhere a little less crowded than our present flat, and it would be nice to pick up some attractive items if we could get them at the right price. How would we travel there, Severin?"

"We shall have to make a fairly early start tomorrow morning. Anatole always comes too, and does the driving. Why don't we pick you up in the Rolls at your flat at, say, eight o'clock? Is that too early? If you intend to do any bidding for lots, make sure you register and are given a numbered card each as soon as you arrive at Sedgwick Manor. I have been to sales run by Barley and Whitchurch, this firm of auctioneers, before, and they have a rule that they take bids only when cards are held up – some other firms respond also to subtle signals from bidders, such as a finger laid by the nose, but B and W decided some while ago that this led to too many misunderstandings, so they now enforce that rule."

"Oh good!" said Melpomene, "I always worry at auctions that if I carelessly scratch my ear I will finish up with an antique oak hallstand or a set of willow-pattern chamber-pots! Thanks, Severin, we'll see you in the morning!"

"Very good!" said Alex, "But we still have some other matters in hand! Marjorie, can you get me Superintendent Wilkinson at Woodhampton, please."

When David answered, Alex asked, "David, you seem to know a number of key policemen across the country – do you know anyone at Northampton? I'll tell you the reason if you do."

"As it happens, Alex, you're in luck once again! When I was at the Police Staff College, preparing for my promotion to Superintendent, I struck up a friendship with another candidate on the senior command course, Gilbert Freeman. I believe he finished up as Chief Superintendent at Northampton, after a spell in Warwick."

"Great, David! What we need is someone bright in his area who can do some detecting for us – we have some dodgy individuals around Northampton we'd like investigated. If Mr Freeman could find us someone really special that would be marvellous. We're working on a case that could involve art forgeries – I'm afraid that's about all I can tell you at the moment, it could have international implications!"

David soon rang back, "There was no problem, Alex. I broached the subject with Gilbert, and he says he has just the person, a young detective-inspector, recently promoted from sergeant, who is very bright and will suit you nicely, especially since she is a woman! Her name is DI Stephanie Walters, and you can reach her either through Northampton CID HQ or directly at her office – that is, when she's there, which isn't all that often, because she's very busy – I'll tell you the numbers in a moment. Gil says she was pushed over in the street and badly bruised by a young tearaway a few days ago, but jumped up and chased and held him until another officer came and gave a hand, so she doesn't seem to be a shrinking violet!"

"That's excellent, David! Thanks very much for all your trouble!" said Alex, "We'll get in touch with her in a day or two – we're both going to be at an estate sale in Berkshire all day tomorrow with our latest client, to get a feel for the art business."

Promptly at eight o'clock, Severin's Rolls was at the door, and Mel and Alex jumped in with alacrity. Less than an hour later they approached the gates of the park surrounding the manor. There was a post with a painted sign – 'Parking for Motors' – at a paddock next to the house, causing Mel to wonder where the parking for horse-carriages might be, so Anatole added the Rolls to the end of the short line of cars that was already there, with even a Pickfords' van, ready for some furniture purchases.

In the entrance of the hall was a trestle table attended by a couple of young men who were asking visitors to register in a large ledger, handing each one a numbered card as they did so. Severin made his entry and was greeted as an old client. The space where Melpomene wrote her name, address and card number was the last line of a page. After that the clerk turned the page and removed a sheet of carbon paper, exposing a page full of the copied entries, then turned again to a fresh page, inserting a new piece of carbon paper so Alex could register.

As Mel and Alex walked away with their cards, Mel murmured, "Did you see what he did with the used carbon, Alex? He just threw it into a wastepaper basket. I think I might go back and try to retrieve them later – they could come in handy – what do you think?"

They found a pair of seats, not too near the front, in the great hall, which had been set up with a lectern and desk at the front.

Chapter 10

As people finished flowing in and taking their seats, the auctioneer took his place at the lectern, while a clerk put several piles of paper on the desk.

"My name is Harold Whitchurch," said the auctioneer, "and I will be conducting the proceedings today. I will make a few announcements on procedure, which will follow established practice. Each lot will be offered in turn, and I will accept bids greater than the reserve price, if any, which I shall make clear. If the reserve price is not met, then that lot will be withdrawn. Further bids will be taken that exceed the current highest bid by a minimum amount which I shall set, until there is no further increase, at which time I will knock down the lot by striking my gavel. When all lots have been knocked down or withdrawn, the sale will conclude. Announcements about procedures for settlement and collection will be made then, but I point out now that only cash or instruments previously approved, such as bank cheques, can be accepted."

"If there are no questions, the sale will proceed. Lot 1, please."

An attendant, dressed in a brown overall coat, held up a framed picture, while the auctioneer gave a brief description, "As described in the catalogue – I would urge bidders to read those descriptions carefully, as I will only summarize them briefly here – Lot 1 is a framed oil painting, a portrait of the Fourth Earl Sedgwick, signed Wilhelm den Haag Strasser. There is a reserve of fifty-five guineas on this lot – who will start the bidding?"

Melpomene and Alex watched fascinated as the sale proceeded. Severin sat impassively through the first few lots, showing interest and bidding only when a landscape in the Flemish style was offered. This prompted a competing bid from a bald-headed man in the second row of seats. Alex had his little notebook ready and wrote down each bidder's number and the amount of his bid. Then Severin bid again and Alex recorded his number and bid, too. When the picture was knocked down to the other bidder, Alex had made a column of eight numbers and bids – four for Severin and four for the successful bidder.

Alex said quietly to Mel, "Ideally, one should record all bids from all buyers, but I think that would be too hard to keep up with. I shall concentrate on those that Severin bids for, I think."

"And I will do the same for anyone who bids against him, even when he is bidding on something else," Melpomene said, "the bald-headed one hasn't shown any interest elsewhere yet – I'm keeping an eye on Severin to see when he sits up and takes notice."

After two hours or so, the auctioneer announced that there would be a twenty-minute break, "If you wish to stretch your legs, ladies and gentlemen, please do so, but I shall resume the sale after that time. A bell will be rung as a reminder. Can I ask you to return to the same seats you are occupying now, please, as it will make my job easier."

By that time, Alex had made records of seven of Severin's attempts, three successful ones, mainly for landscapes from various periods, and four similar pictures which he had lost, interestingly three of them to the bald-headed man and the other to a fat man dressed in corduroys, looking like a farmer.

Melpomene had recorded another four purchases made by the bald-headed man, taking details also for the unsuccessful bidders in each case, all different. The fat farmer had shown no further interest in any other lots.

"I'm going to stretch my legs, wink, wink!" said Mel, and left the hall, saying to an attendant, "Could you direct me to the ladies' lavatory, please?"

She disappeared in the direction indicated, but had a good look at the trestle table near the entrance doors. There was no sign of the waste-paper basket, so she looked around on her way to the lavatory. Sure enough, there was a door leading outside, and beyond that – some dustbins. She tried two and than struck pay-dirt – there was a crumpled bundle of carbon paper in the top of the third, which she took with her into the ladies', shutting herself in a cubicle.

She carefully separated the sheets of paper, trying not to mark them any further, and made a stack which she folded carefully and put into her handbag.

Just then the bell sounded and she walked back into the auction room and took her seat next to Alex, nudging him and smiling.

After the break, matters proceeded much as before, and the two made several further records. Interestingly, the bald-headed man had outbid Severin and two other buyers on a dozen further occasions, and seemed to be rather more successful than most. As Alex said, "He has committed himself for quite a sum – I wonder if he has it – he doesn't impress me as being a man of wealth! Maybe he is bidding on behalf of someone else."

"Has Severin been successful at all?" asked Mel, "I have been too busy watching baldy to keep track."

"Oh yes, he has bought another two pictures, I think. He doesn't look particularly happy about things! Look, Mel, while the settling up is going on, keep an eye on your bald-headed friend. When he has finished and leaves, why don't see if you can follow him surreptitiously and find out whether he meets anyone. I still think he may have been buying for someone else. I'll go and commiserate with Severin once he has settled."

As they thought, Severin was not a particularly happy man. When Alex questioned him he almost snapped, "I reckon they've been running a ring against me! I've come across this before, but haven't been stung myself, fortunately. What happens is that a few shady dealers get together and agree not to bid against each other, but instead one of them tries to secure lots at the lowest possible price. For the buying public at large, it is the thrill of competition which drives them to greater and greater bids – I suppose you could say it is a form of gambling, and we know how that can grip people. Then, Alex, they get together and split up the proceeds between them, sometimes by running a sort of secondary auction – so they have got themselves some nice bargains! Of course it is highly illegal! Look, here comes Melpomene! What has she been up to? She looks like the cat who got into the cream!"

Mel drew them both aside, and in a conspiratorial whisper said, "Come with me to the car park!"

She led them there and pointed to the Pickfords pantechnicon, from which the others could hear a lot of shouting and banging on the sides.

"I followed Baldy, and he was laughing and backslapping with a bunch of his cronies in the back of the van. So I slammed the back door, put down the bolts and trapped them! Then I went to the house and called the police. They should get here very soon!"

Chapter 11

"Oh, well done, Melpomene!" exclaimed Severin, "But what made you think they had done something illegal?"

"They said so!" replied Mel, "The bald one slapped another one's back and bragged that the coppers wouldn't catch them now, and that anyway he had given a false name as they had all agreed to do beforehand. Another said, 'All we gotta do now is load the loot into the van!' to which Baldy replied 'Don't go calling it that, we bought it fair and square!', laughing like mad. That was when I slammed the door on them and shot the bolts!"

A police car and a Black Maria van drove up soon after, and an inspector got out and approached them, saying, "I'm Inspector Thorpe of Reading police. Where will I find Melpemmy Crabbe?"

"That's me, but it's really Melpomene!" said Mel, and the policeman saluted and said, "Sorry, madam, the lad who took the call isn't familiar with foreign names. I'll get my men to deal with these gentlemen – we can all hear where they are at the moment – and then I would like to talk to the auctioneer – Mr Whitchurch, isn't it?"

They all went into the auction room, where most of the audience were still waiting for settlement to begin, and the inspector explained the situation to Mr Whitchurch. After a short discussion with the inspector and another gentleman, the auctioneer made a general announcement.

"Ladies and gentlemen, I am somewhat embarrassed to have to tell you that our sale has been affected by irregular, even criminal, activities. My clerks and I need to peruse our records – we naturally make a full notation of every sale – to find out which lots were affected. The legal position is that when it is found that illegal bidding has occurred, those bids are declared null and void and the goods are returned to the vendor. And then, if the vendor agrees – as the legal representative of this estate has decided to do in this case – the highest unaffected legal bid is accepted. So please bear with us, ladies and gentlemen, and if you are one of those who might have lost your bidding to one or other of the wrong-doers, you might find you are lucky after all! Of course, all those who made successful first bids are unaffected by any of this!"

A police sergeant came up and had a few words with Inspector Thorpe, handing him some auction cards, which he passed to the auctioneer, saying, "My sergeant has noted who was holding which card but maybe they haven't divulged their real names yet."

Whitchurch read out the four numbers, saying, "If any unsuccessful bidder recognizes any of these as one which outbid him or her, please tell me and this will save us some time. We will, of course, make an exhaustive check later in confirmation."

Melpomene told Severin, "The ringleader, who I've been calling 'Baldy' is number 227. I think he pipped you several times, so you may be going home with a better haul than you thought!"

Indeed, a couple or three hours later, Anatole drove the Rolls up to the front of the DuPlessis gallery, saying, "Now we can unload the spoils! The advantage of a Rolls limousine like this is that when the occasional seats are folded up, there is space for quite a few pictures! Pity we had to leave the big pair of seascapes to be sent on by lorry!"

Severin was very pleased to be home with his haul, and when they had all helped to carry the pictures into the gallery, to cries of admiration from Sandy, he embraced Melpomene and said, "Unless you two sleuths have anything else on the boil, let me treat you to an appropriate dinner! You, too, Sandy – I think I could get used to your new name!"

Then Alex said, "While we are all feeling triumphant, I would like to show all you a trifle I picked up, too. I'm glad to report that nobody bid against me on this one, and Melpomene was so busy taking notes of Severin's attempts that she missed my only transaction. Here, my dear this is for you!"

He handed Melpomene a small object wrapped in tissue paper, which she tore open to reveal a pair of green drop earrings! She hugged and kissed Alex until he started to blush, and protested, "They are only paste, my darling, but they look close enough to emeralds to create an impressive show when you wish to be the centre of attention!"

"Might I use your telephone, Severin?" he went on, "Marjorie is probably still at the office, so I'd like to see if there has been any action there while we've been away."

Marjorie was indeed still there, and Alex asked if there had been any telephone calls, "We're still waiting for something from Jens-Olle Pedersen, of course!"

"Better than that!" said Marjorie, "He dropped in, in person! Not to worry about missing him, though, he said it was only on the off-chance, and he has left me contact numbers, not only for here, where he'll be for two or three days, but also for Copenhagen! I told him how pleased you'd both be about that, and he said that he had needed to check with his colleagues before getting their permission to disclose it. Do you want those numbers now?"

"No, no, thanks, Marjorie – we're off to dinner now – Severin's treat. We've had a very interesting day today, in more than one sense! We'll tell you all about it in the morning. Anything else?"

"Only some summonses! No – don't panic, you haven't perpetrated any offences – these are just to command you both to appear at the Old Bailey for some murder trial or other! Not for a while yet. Apart from that, nothing but a few minor bills."

Severin invited everyone to his office for a pre-dinner drink, having got Anatole to reserve a table at a restaurant he often patronized, saying, "They have music there, but none of your noisy jazz stuff, just a piano trio specializing in French light music."

It did turn out to be very pleasant, accompanied by a selection of appropriate wines, all of which Severin insisted on paying for, since he had had such a profitable day at the sale, "Mostly due to the good offices of Crabbe and Crabbe!" he said, quaffing another glass of good French champagne.

Alex said, "It is we who should be grateful to you, Severin, for introducing us to an area of criminality that we were oblivious of before today!" And they all toasted this too.

It was quite late before cabs were called for and Alex and Melpomene arrived at the flat just a little the worse for wear. Caroline and Mrs M were well asleep by then, so the couple made as little commotion as possible before having their baths and collapsing into bed.

Chapter 12

Melpomene and Alex went to the office straight after breakfast, as Alex was keen to renew contact with Jens-Olle. He greeted Marjorie and was about to ask her to ring him, when Melpomene had a thought.

"It would be nice to have some information for him about the auction ring gang," she said, "but we don't yet know their proper names – they bragged about giving false ones when they registered for the auction. Let's ring that Inspector Thorpe and ask him – even dubious characters like that must know it is an offence to give false names to the police! Can you get Inspector Thorpe at Reading police, please, Marjorie?"

After a few delays, as the enquiry was passed from department to department, Inspector Thorpe answered – Melpomene took the receiver, while Alex picked up the other earpiece.

"Good morning, Inspector, Melpomene Crabbe here! How have you got on with your catch from yesterday – we were just wondering, have you found out their real names yet?"

"Hello, thanks for ringing – yes we have, I'm happy to say. The one calling himself Burton is really an old customer, we even have his prints on file, his name is Keith Satterfield. I can tell you the others' too, because once Satterfield had faded they all followed suit."

"Oh, good, Inspector – actually the name Satterfield rings a bell with us, I believe – I will double-check with Alex – it is certainly quite unusual. Can you tell me their auction numbers too? We know that Satterfield, aka Burton, was 227. "

"Just a moment – can you pass me that buff folder, Constable – here we are – Satterfield, 227, as you say, and then we have Henry Arthur Winton, 229, calling himself Jones – Andrew Liversedge, 310, calling himself Smith – and Martin Wilmot, 332, calling himself Brown. What creative imaginations some of these crims have! A policeman would have been suspicious of those names straight away, but I suppose sale-room clerks are not as inclined to be sensitive! Is that what you were looking for, Melpomene?"

"Yes, indeed, Inspector! Thank you very much! May we bother you again if we need anything more?"

"No bother at all – I'm always prepared to cooperate with anyone on my side of the frontier!"

"Very interesting!" said Mel, ringing off, "It looks as though we have stumbled upon one of Mildred Henderson's dinner guests! I have never come across a Satterfield before, so it would be strange if there were two different people of that name, both interested in art! So now we have an even better reason to try to talk to Jens-Olle. Can you oblige, please, Marjorie – you have his number of course – did he tell you where he would be this morning and whether he would be busy?"

When Jens-Olle answered, Melpomene asked whether he had the time to talk to her and Alex about a few things, to which he replied, "Would it not be better for me to come to your office? I have an ulterior motive – the tea and coffee they serve here are execrable, making me long for a cup of your Lapsang Souchong. May I come? I think it will only take me a few minutes, I have a car and driver at my disposal."

"Please come, by all means! – do you like jam tarts?"

The kettle was boiling when Jens-Olle arrived, so he was soon in a receptive mood.

Said Melpomene, "We have a number of matters to report, Jens-Olle, arising since you left London last time. We have no real idea of their value to you, but here goes. First, accompanied by Alex Mainwaring, a water-colour expert employed by Severin DuPlessis, I paid a visit to the Hendersons in Northampton to talk about Postlethwaite's denunciation of their aquarelle. We talked with Henderson's wife, Mildred, who said that Postlethwaite looked to her to be hatching something up with a group of his allies. We got their names, thinking that although Postlethwaite himself didn't ring any alarm bells, some of the others might. I have written the names down, and I will give it to you."

"This is a good approach, Melpomene!" said Jens-Olle, "Our organization is trying to put together all its information in ways that let us see patterns developing, much like the approach used by social anthropologists, as you pointed out to me."

"You're right!" she agreed, "And yesterday we had an even more interesting day at an estate sale that Severin took us to. I'm sure in your work, Jens-Olle, that you will have come across the so-called auction ring – perhaps in Denmark it has another name?"

"If you mean the scheme where a group of dishonest buyers agree not to bid against each other, thus obtaining bargains, which they then auction privately among themselves, yes indeed! We call it an 'ulovlig hemmelige auktion' – so did you see such a ring in action?"

"We did indeed!" aid Mel, "Not only did we see it, but we caught them at it, and had them arrested by the police!"

"Mel is too modest!" said Alex, "She captured these four reprobates single-handedly, by trapping them in the van they had brought to take away their spoils! They are now locked up and awaiting trial! And what's more, one of them has the same name – Satterfield – as one of the group at the Henderson's fateful dinner party. We haven't checked that he is the same person, but Satterfield is not a very common name!"

"So here we are, Jens-Olle," said Mel, "the group at the Hendersons' was Postlethwaite, Barker, Perkins, Benson and Satterfield, and the auction conspirators were Satterfield once again, Winton, Liversedge and Wilmot. We have the full names and addresses of the auction lot – Satterfield for one was already known by the police, having been convicted before – I could find out for you if you want. Or I could give you Inspector Thorpe's number at Reading police station."

"I'd prefer not to make myself known to him," said Jens-Olle, "the fewer people who know me, the more secure will my investigation be. But I shall certainly pass on all these names to my bureau. It is very intriguing to me that there is apparently a connection between those trying to discredit the Duplessis Gallery and drive down the value of Mr Henderson's aquarelle and those running the ring – which again would have damaged Mr DuPlessis' business, had it succeeded."

"Couldn't it just be a coincidence that he has been affected by two separate enterprises?" asked Alex.

"I have come to believe, Alex," said Jens-Olle, "that there is no such thing as a coincidence in this business – once we disentangle this complex web, we will probably see that every part of it is the design of a master-mind. I shall now share with you both some of the results of my own detective work!"

Chapter 13

"As soon as I got back to Copenhagen last time," Jens-Olle said, "I went to talk to my colleagues about the slanderous remarks made about the 'Daphnis and Chloe' picture. At that time I had not heard of Mrs Henderson's speculations about her other dinner guests, so all we had to go on was the name Postlethwaite – a thorough search of the files for that proved fruitless. I had even suggested that they try a few misspellings – as I said before, it is a difficult name for Danes to pronounce, and so there could have been mistakes in transcription – but this brought no further results. So I suggested to them that we follow a different tack, rather than just getting frustrated over that name."

"Maybe when you add in the extra names we have just given to you, your colleagues can reopen that hunt," suggested Alex, "but forgive me for interrupting – what new line did you take?"

"I suggested we look for patterns. With the Daphnis and Chloe, we had a case of someone throwing doubt on the authenticity of the work to achieve some illicit end or other, so we could try to find instances of similar behaviour. In our group we have a young detective who is a part-time postgraduate student in Art History at the Royal Danish Academy of Fine Arts, so he is used to research techniques as well as being fascinated by the arts. So I took him aside and we worked out a plan of campaign together, involving searching materials held both at the Academy's Charlottenborg Palace and at central police records in Copenhagen. In my judgment, he will be meticulous – he will report back only to me."

Melpomene sat up at this, "Your mention of a young assistant reminds me that we have been given the name of a keen young female detective in the Northampton police, Detective-Inspector Stephanie Walters. Our initial thought was that she could have a keen look at Postlethwaite and his cohorts – we haven't spoken to her yet – but it now occurs to me that she could also run a parallel enquiry to that of your assistant through the centralized police files held at Scotland Yard. Maybe you could pave the way for her, Jens-Olle, with your contacts there. If you prefer not to make direct contact with her, we can speak to her on your behalf and explain the approach."

"And I think," said Alex, "we should not rule out cases of actual rather than suspected forgery, or even out-and-out theft of art works, either, since we could expect that those engaged in one type of illicit activity would also indulge in others."

Then Alex remembered something, "Mel, we haven't looked at the carbon copies of the registrations at the sale yet. Do you think we might get some more information from them? They would certainly confirm what we know about the spurious bidding against Severin, but that group, or indeed others for that matter – though I don't know how we could tell – could also have been targeting other buyers. The auctioneer, Mr Whitchurch, explained at the time how people could check their own purchases, but we didn't follow any of this up ourselves – unless you did, Mel?"

"No. I didn't – I was rather full of the drama of the moment at that time! When I get a chance I will go through them. Marjorie might help me sort it all out – she is good at paper-work! And we should speak to Mr Whitchurch – he must have come across similar cases in the past."

Jens-Olle had been sitting and listening to all this, with an occasional nod of his head, and now he spoke up.

"I am not so familiar with the scene in this country, of course, but in Denmark, and in France, too, I believe, auctioneers and art dealers have a guild or association through which they exchange information. For example, they circulate black-lists of buyers whom they wish to ban from their sale-rooms. I was surprised to hear that Satterfield had been convicted before – in my country this would have automatically put him on the black list!"

"But," said Alex, "He was using a false name, so unless he was recognised by any of the auctioneer's staff, how would they know that he was banned?"

"Ah, that is indeed a difficulty!" said Jens-Olle, "None of our three countries has an official government-issued identity card, so it would not be easy for an auctioneer to insist on proof of identity! Maybe we should push for their introduction – it would be a great help for the police, too!"

"And that," said Alex, "is the very reason that Great Britain does not have such a document! It would be considered even by upright citizens as an infringement of civil liberties!"

Melpomene broke in, "Whatever the circumstances – and we could go on arguing about this for a long time on philosophical and moral grounds – I still think it would be a good idea to approach Mr Whitchurch. He might welcome further contact, and we could find out about guilds or associations that might be very valuable for us in this and other cases!"

That seemed to each of them to be a good time to stop talking and get on separately with planning some action, so they had farewell cups of tea all round.

"Will you come to a restaurant and have a meal with us, Jens-Olle?" asked Melpomene, but he politely demurred, saying that he should get back to the department before much longer, as he had more discussions scheduled with colleagues from France and England, who were all gathering in London for one of their periodic plenary sessions.

"Oh, is Hugo Palance going to be there?" asked Mel, "I would very much like to see him again if he can find an opportunity soon."

"Of course!" said Jens-Olle, "How foolish of me to forget about it – he has mentioned more than once that he would like to meet you again and also be introduced to Alex. I will have a word with him this afternoon, and he will probably get in touch. I have no need of a taxi this time, since my official driver can be here in a few minutes, if I may use your telephone, please."

"Or," said Alex, "I can easily run you there in our Alvis."

"Forgive me for appearing paranoid," said Jens-Olle, "but once again I must avoid establishing any connection that could be used by our antagonists."

"I can understand completely!" replied Alex, "We have taken precautions before to conceal from the ungodly our association with such a distinctive car as our bright red Alvis, which has the power to turn any head!"

While they waited, they chatted about trivia, including their various visits to the cinema, finding that Jens-Olle was a fan of Scandinavian stars, including Greta Garbo, of course, and other continental actresses, like Pola Negri, the Polish star of many popular German films, and of other German films, such as 'Siegfried', 'The Cabinet of Dr Caligari' and 'Nosferatu'. Mel made Jens-Olle promise to see a picture with them before long.

Chapter 14

After breakfast, Melpomene said, "I'll just telephone the office and let Marjorie know we shall be in soon to make a lot of calls."

She rang the number and waited, " 'No answer was the stern reply!' " she said, "I wonder where Marjorie has got to?"

"Maybe she's simply in the lavatory, or doing some shopping," said Alex, "just give her a few minutes."

Mel tried after ten minutes, with no result, then again after half an hour. "I think we'd better go!" she said, "maybe she will have left us a note – but I'm surprised she didn't telephone."

They parked as usual, and Melpomene popped into Mrs Jenkins' shop, "Have you seen Marjorie this morning?" she asked, and Mrs Jenkins shook her head and said to her little assistant, "You ain't seen Miss Wentworth today 'ave you, Phyllis?" She shook her head, and the shopkeeper went on, "I dunno what's up, Madam, but you may as well take the tarts what I put aside for you, anyway."

The office door was still locked, and there were no signs inside that Marjorie had been there.

"I'm getting worried!" said Melpomene, "I'm wondering all sorts of things – she's been kidnapped by an art gang, or she has lost her memory, or had an accident – what shall we try first, Alex?"

"Let's call the local hospital first, Mel, that would cover two of your three!"

He looked in the telephone book for the number, and then rang it, "Good morning, Alexander Crabbe here, could you transfer me to admissions or emergency, please – we think our secretary, Miss Marjorie Wentworth, might have met with an accident."

The person he was talking to said, "We keep a list of recent admissions by the switchboard – this lets us answer a lot of enquiries very quickly. Let me see, yes, M. Wentworth – minor injuries, she is in a recovery room after receiving treatment. She is not on a ward yet, so the normal visiting hours don't apply, you can come and see her straight away. Use the Trott Street entrance."

The hospital was within easy walking distance, so they were soon at the Trott St enquiries desk. "Wentworth, Wentworth – yes, here we are! Follow that corridor, then first left and you will find a nurse's station where you can ask."

They were shown into a recovery room and saw Marjorie, lying on a bed, not under the covers, with both hands heavily bandaged.

Melpomene embraced her – carefully – asking, "What on earth have you been doing to yourself, my dear – we were worried sick!"

"Oh, Mel, I feel so stupid – I came off my bike! But I suppose it wasn't really my fault – a dog ran out and I swerved and hit the kerb! Next I knew I was lying on the gravel pavement with both hands bleeding! They've picked out all the bits and put ointment on and they say I can go home as soon as I feel ready. I don't think I'll be using my hands for three or four days, though! Oh, I'm so sorry, Mel and Alex!"

"Now don't go blaming yourself, Marjorie! We can cope! When you're ready we'll run you home and your Mum can look after you until you're completely better!"

On the way to Marjorie's home, Mel travelled in the dicky seat while Marjorie sat by Alex so he could follow her directions. Then she said, "You should go to Prescott's Agency in our High Street, that's where I went when my previous job ended. They're very good – they found you two for me, didn't they – and they will fix you up with a temp, who can always telephone me at home if she needs to sort anything out – ooh, I must give you my home number – it's not written down at work anywhere."

At Marjorie's place, one in a terrace of identical houses, Mrs Wentworth fussed over her daughter, saying, "Don't try to use your hands, I'll help you! Where is your bicycle now? It was a good one, wasn't it?" "Don't worry, Mum, I had my accident outside Mr Norris' greengrocers' shop and he called the ambulance and said he would look after my bike until I could pick it up!"

Then Mrs Wentworth made cups of tea all round. "Marjorie tells me you only have nice tea at your office, so I got in some

44

Typhoo – I hope you like that one! And I've got some Garibaldi biscuits!"

Mel and Alex gratefully accepted, realizing that they had got rather worked up about everything and needed to relax a little.

Matters went smoothly at Prescott's employment agency, and soon Melpomene and Alex had engaged a new temporary assistant, Winifred Morris, brought her to the office and were explaining the job to her. As she was being shown her desk and typewriter, she told them she was a graduate of Pitman's College. "Like Marjorie!" said Melpomene, "Where do you live, Winifred?"

"Call me Winnie, please! I'm only fifteen minutes' walk from here, sharing a flat with two other girls, so it works out very well. I was working for a dentist until recently, but he really needed a qualified assistant, not a secretary, so it didn't last. And before that I was working for an estate agent, but the housing market is getting very tight, so they didn't need as many staff. I hope I can learn what you want me to do very quickly, because I don't suppose I shall be needed here for very long either. A pity, because it would be nice to have a more permanent position, and this sounds like an interesting job!"

"Maybe it gets a little too interesting at times!" said Alex, "And I have an idea that we may be able to find more work for you, if we like your style! We sometimes have several irons in the fire at the same time – we shall see!"

"Now one of your most important jobs is answering the telephone," he went on, "and if one or both of us are here, you can call us to pick up the call in the back office. Of course, if we are not about, apologize and take a detailed message. This must be standard office procedure that you know already, so forgive me for treating you like a beginner!"

"Oh, no, Mr Crabbe, I would prefer you did, rather than leave me to make my own assumptions that I might get all wrong!"

Melpomene added, "You'll see, by the side of the telephone, a little index book. This has all the important telephone numbers, names and addresses in it, and a short description sometimes of who they are. If you speak to someone who is not already in it, please take their details and add them. This is possibly the most important article in the office – apart from you or Marjorie, that is!"

Chapter 15

"Now, Winnie," Mel went on, "before all this drama with Marjorie happened, we were going to make several important telephone calls – so you can take Marjorie's place, it will be a good learning experience for you. First, please get me Mr Whitchurch, he's an auctioneer – I will watch, and listen on the other earpiece while you do it this time, so you needn't be nervous. After this one, you'll be on your own!"

Without hesitation, Winnie reached for the telephone index, flipped through to the W's, picked up the telephone and asked for the number. The operator answered, "That will be a toll call, Madam, will you proceed?" Winnie said, "Yes, I will," and when the call was picked up, said, "Could I speak to Mr Whitchurch, please, I am calling for Melpomene Crabbe ... Mr Whitchurch? Just a moment, please, here is Melpomene Crabbe." Then she called to Mel, "Here is your call to Mr Whitchurch, you can take it in the back office!"

Melpomene gave Winnie the thumbs up, handed the second earpiece to Alex, went and picked up the phone and was soon talking to Whitchurch.

"Hello, Mr Whitchurch, remember me?"

"How could I forget you, Melpomene? Every time I think of that day, I can't help grinning like a Cheshire cat. I have to go to the court hearing for their charges in a day or two, and I shall enjoy that too!"

"It was rather good, wasn't it? The reason I called you was to ask you whether you belong to any sort of guild or association of auctioneers – I just heard from an acquaintance that such bodies exist in other countries. In particular, I was told that they might maintain black-lists of buyers caught behaving in unacceptable or even criminal ways."

"I can follow your reasoning, Melpomene, and I can confirm that there are such bodies here and our firm is a member of at least two of them, but we have found it very hard to work any system of black-lists – we would need to keep photographs of all those listed, or tattoo a warning symbol on their foreheads or something, since England has no system of government identity cards or the like."

"Exactly the conclusion we have come to ourselves, Harold – may I call you Harold? – so do you have other ways of keeping track of dishonesty of various kinds?"

"Of course, we do see familiar faces again and again – there are art-sale enthusiasts just as there are sports fans – so if we suspected anybody we recognized, we would keep a special watch on him or her. But this is hardly systematic or comprehensive – it's very much a matter of luck! As it happens, at that same auction where you had all the fun, I was keeping my eye on a lady I've seen many times before!"

"Oh, that's interesting!" said Melpomene, "Tell me more, do!"

"She is quite distinctive in appearance – tall, sharp distinguished features, white hair in a bun, no hat, usually wears a fox stole over an expensive-looking cloth coat. She writes notes in a little book all the time, but I've never seen her bid for anything, not even once – she never registers so she wouldn't be able to bid anyway – so Lord knows why she comes! She doesn't look like a student, somehow – we do get art-history students and those from art schools quite often – I encourage them and I even go and give talks at colleges from time to time."

"Are we talking about estate and country-house sales only, or does this woman turn up at your sale-rooms as well?"

"Every time, Melpomene! I and my partner, Gordon Barley, have been in business for ten years now and I would say she has not missed a single one of our sales for, let me think, over five years! She turns up in a chauffeur-driven car and as soon as the last lot has been offered, she is up and off, so I've never been able to exchange even a word with her – I call her 'Lady Mysterious'."

"Very intriguing, Harold – you've started my detecting whiskers twitching! When is your next sale?"

"Why, tomorrow, Mel, at our sale-rooms on Kings Road, Reading, near the central library. We're offering a selection of pictures that we've had around the place for a long time, as well as a collection of the work of two aspiring local artists. In house, we refer to this as our 'jumble sale' – but I wouldn't use that term in public, of course! Viewing starts at nine o'clock, and the sale commences at 11.30 – so you're thinking of coming, Mel?"

"I certainly am, Harold! Could Alex and I check in with you during the viewing period? Then you can point out 'Lady Mysterious' for us."

"She normally turns up only just before the sale itself, but I can tip one of you the wink when she does – but you could probably pick her out from my description anyway – and I will enjoy chatting with you both. See you tomorrow!"

Mel and Alex both hung up, and Mel said to Winnie, "Well done, Winnie, and now for your second most important task at Crabbe and Crabbe – please make a pot of Lapsang Souchong tea, with cups for three – I hope you like that sort, Winnie – and break out the jam tarts, since we now have an important conference!"

Alex said, "Let me guess, Mel, this is going to be a quest to identify this mysterious lady, is it not? I volunteer to work on the chauffeur and the car, while you tackle the lady herself – how about that for a start?"

"Of course, we will have to play a lot of it by ear," said Mel, "while I think of it, make sure you have coins in your pocket for a phone box, and the number of Mile End Road police station, then you can ask Jimmy or one of his people to look up the registration number of the car. Maybe you can engage the chauffeur in conversation, Alex, he could be a useful source of information."

Winnie was sitting listening to all this, with her eyes sparkling and a jam tart poised halfway to her mouth.

Alex noticed this, and decided to give her even more of a thrill, so he said to Mel, "And I'd better make sure I've got plenty of ammunition for my Luger pistol, too – you never know when it might be useful!"

But Melpomene thought this was taking it too far, so she patted Winnie on the arm and said, "This time, he is only kidding, Winnie! This agency only occasionally has to deal with kidnappers, murderers and other violent types – why it must be more than a week since last time, isn't that right, Alex?"

Winnie was quick to pick up the mood, "I must remember to pack my black-jack, my stiletto and my garrotting wire in my handbag next time I come to work!"

There was laughter all round.

Chapter 16

They found the Barley and Whitchurch sale-rooms in Reading quite easily, parked the Alvis in a laneway by the side of the building just before 9 o'clock, and walked round to the foyer, where they each took a sale catalogue from a pile. There were only a few buyers or spectators so far, wandering about in the gallery space with their catalogues, looking at the pictures that had taken their fancy.

Harold Whitchurch was talking to a couple by the doors into the sale-room, but excused himself when he spotted Melpomene and Alex and came over to greet them. "The registration desk is just inside," he said, "Will you register and take numbers?"

"Oh yes," said Mel, "we want to be just like the other buyers here, and avoid attracting attention. So I'll find something in the catalogue now and pretend to discuss it with you. Are there any lots that you anticipate will attract high bids?"

"Even we seasoned auctioneers cannot always predict these things," said Harold, "but I have high hopes of one or two quite old Flemish-style portraits in oils, and there is a huge Victorian hunting scene that the vendor, a local squire, has set a high reserve on, which maybe we'll be able to achieve if the right buyers are here today."

"Any news of you-know-who?" asked Alex, "Does she get dropped at the door, or is her car usually parked near by?"

"It varies, I'm afraid. She comes to all of our sales – she was at our exciting Sedgwick Manor sale for instance, and we shall definitely see her today. Anyway, wander about, please – I have to make myself pleasant to the members of the throng! Keep your eyes open after about 11 am, and you will probably spot her."

"Thanks, Harold," said Alex, "I shall loiter around, and with any luck I'll spot her arriving. I really want to see where her car gets parked, so I can casually approach the driver, and see what information I can wheedle out of him."

In the event, they nearly missed her, mainly because she was wearing a full-length fur coat instead of a fox stole, but Harold waved to them just in time. Alex then made a bee-line for the door and saw a large black limousine pull away from the kerb and drive away! Fortunately, however, he saw the car stop outside a coffee shop a hundred yards or so up the street.

He walked quickly to the café and went in. A man with a chauffeur's cap was ordering at the counter, so Alex went and stood by him, rubbing his hands together, saying, "Getting a bit colder, these days, eh?"

The chauffeur said, not unpleasantly, "If you drive an expensive car you don't have to worry about cold hands or feet!"

"Can I join you?" said Alex, "What's the coffee like here? Those apple pies look all right, I think I'll risk one!"

As the man made no objection, they both sat at a table near the window. Alex nodded towards the limousine, visible just outside, "That your car?" he asked, "or your employer's I should say, I suppose!"

"Sort of," the man said with a snort, "it belongs to 'Robinson's Hire Cars and Hearses' – fortunately I never have to drive a hearse! I have a regular client who I drive a couple or three times a week – she's quiet but not as quiet as those would be! I just took her to the art auction – she must really like them, seeing how many she goes to! Never ever buys anything, as far as I can see, but maybe she has them delivered. Lives in a big house in Richmond, she does."

"So she must be rich – is she Lady something?"

"Nah! Just Mrs Eliza Stanford – and if you heard her speak you'd know she's no lady! Her friend's a bit rough, too! I have to take her to his place on her way home every time – she doesn't go in, she just rings the bell, and when he comes out they have a chat and she gives him something. Once or twice they've had a row on the doorstep – shouting like a couple of fishwives! I don't take no notice, though."

"Doesn't sound like a Richmond type, that man!" commented Alex.

"His place is in Hounslow – and not the posh parts, neither! Why are you so interested, anyway – you'll be wanting my life-history next! Newspaper man, are you?"

"Not at all!" said Alex, "But I write short stories, so I'm always on the look-out for interesting tales. Every now and again, a magazine will pick one up, but not as often as I'd like, so I'll have to go on being a door-to-door salesman for a while! Encyclopedias, you know. Well, it's been nice talking to you, I must get back to my wife at the sale – she's fond of pictures, but we can't afford to buy many. Are you just going to hang about for your passenger?"

"No, I'll settle down in the back of the car and see if I can have a snooze! She won't bother if she catches me asleep, she's used to it!"

Back at the salerooms, the auction was well under way. Alex saw that Melpomene had kept a seat for him in the third row, so he made his way quietly and sat down. Mrs Stanford was in the row in front, making notes in a little black book.

Harold Whitchurch was just coming to the next lot.

"Lot 12, a collection of six little water-colours of floral subjects, ladies and gentlemen. Amateur work, of course, but they would enhance any room. Shall we start with ten guineas?"

Alex saw that Mrs Stanford was even making notes about such a relatively minor item. He murmured to Mel, "Any signs of dubious bidding?" but she shook her head, saying, "Afterwards, Alex – we don't want people shushing us!"

From the point of view of Crabbe and Crabbe, there was nothing of particular interest in the remainder of the sale. When the audience started to break up, Mrs Stanford headed for the door, where her limousine was already waiting.

Alex and Mel walked quickly to the Alvis, with Alex averting his face as they passed the limousine, but he saw that the chauffeur was busily settling his passenger and would not have seen him in any case.

Alex took the wheel, saying, "I found out roughly where they are going, Mel, so we don't have to follow them very closely, just make sure to keep them in sight. When they stop at a certain house in Hounslow, I shall just drive past, but see if you can make a note of the house number and the street name. If there are any particular landmarks, make a note of them too."

As predicted, the limousine stopped at a grubby house in a grubby street. They pulled up a few yards further on, and watched until the woman made her report and the limousine set off again. Then, "Wimbledon, ho!" Alex said.

Chapter 17

The house in Wimbledon was certainly quite large and imposing. As they drove by they could see the woman getting out of the car at the front steps. There were no gates, just a gravel drive round a circle of flower-beds. They stopped the Alvis, and as they looked back, they could see that the limousine was setting off the way they had come.

"Shall we follow it?" said Melpomene, but Alex answered. "Not much point, I already know the car belongs to a commercial fleet. We can look it up at any time, it's called 'Robinson's Hire Cars and Hearses'. I'm more interested in that place in Hounslow at the moment. It's still fairly early, so do you feel like a little bit of sleuthing there?"

Now that there was no longer any need to keep vigilant, Alex related what the chauffeur had told him, "He must get quite bored on that job, he told me a lot without needing much prompting. My first thoughts are that dear Eliza is providing a gang of some sort with information about who buys what. Maybe they are specialist burglars who deal in art works only!"

"If so," said Melpomene, "it might be worth our while to see if there are any records of art thefts in this area over the last five years – didn't Harold say that she had been regularly turning up over that period?"

"Newspaper files might help, if someone has been organized enough to keep them sorted in useful ways. Or else the police, of course. How are we going to proceed at this Hounslow house, Mel – we shall be there soon – here's that pub, the Fox and Geese, that we noticed on the corner of the street as we left. Will you just go to the door and play it sort of straight – what are you thinking?"

"Well, first I've noticed that you've automatically concluded that it'll be me making this approach – not that I mind! What I shall do is play the role of, shall we say, an estate agent. They can be pretty nosy! And you, Alex, can stay out of sight for now in case we need you as a second string, OK? Park out of sight, and I'll just walk up. I've got my bundle of notes I took at the auction – estate agents always have something with them."

Melpomene rang the bell, and when the man opened it, said brightly, "Mr Stevenson? I'm from Whitley and Stafford, estate agents in the town. We were told that you are interested in putting the house on the market."

"You must 'ave it wrong, Miss, my name is Odgers and there ain't nobody called Stevenson 'ere. You sure they didn't say Stevens? – We got a Stevens, but e's just a tenant like the rest of us, and e's an 'alf-wit, anyhow! It's me what always answers the bell, because my rooms are just at the front 'ere."

"Oh, what a pity, Mr Odgers," said Mel, in her best tragic voice, with her face lowered, looking at the man prettily through her eyelashes, "I've walked so far this afternoon already. Do you think I could come in and look around a bit, so I've at least got something to tell my manager? He's going to shout at me anyway, but that might help!"

"Well, I dunno, Miss – oh all right, step inside. It ain't much, as you'll see, and I can't show you anybody's rooms, so I can't see as it'll be much 'elp. There's two flats, or rooms, really – we all share the lavs and so on, on each floor. It's Mr Dodds you really want to see, 'e's the owner, but 'e on'y turns up of a Friday, when the rent's due. The agents are Wilson and Pickett, they'd be able to put you on to 'im."

Just then there was a ring on the bell, and Odgers almost ran to answer it. Melpomene could not hear any of the conversation that ensued, but Odgers went into his room and came out with what Mel could see was a notebook, handed it through the door to the visitor and shut the door behind him.

"That's about all I can show you, Miss. As you see, it ain't much of a place!"

"Thank you anyway, Mr Odgers, you've been as helpful as you could, I'm sure. Good day!"

She walked back along the road to where Alex was waiting in the Alvis and got in. "Did you just see someone come to the house?' she asked. "I did, and I wrote his number down, as I did with Mrs Stanford's limousine, but he drove off so smartly I knew we wouldn't be able to catch him. So did you find out anything in there?"

Mel told him the little she had learned, and they decided that there was no point in hanging around so they might as well go back to the office. When they got there it was quite a bit past their usual closing time, but Winnie was still there waiting for them.

"That's very good of you, Winnie," said Alex, "but in future you should lock up and go home at a reasonable time, otherwise you could be waiting for us till all hours. Any visitors or telephone calls?"

"Yes, Mr Crabbe, a gentleman came and said he was looking for someone who could help him sort out a dispute he was having with a neighbour. I said that it wasn't up to me to take on any new jobs, but I wrote down his particulars and said you would get in touch. Was this the right thing to do?"

"Certainly, Winnie, that was very good. Call me Alex, by the way!"

"And there were two telephone calls from the police – I wrote them down, let's see. Detective Sergeant Manley, he said you would know how to reach him, and a lady, Detective Inspector Walters, of the Northampton Constabulary. Could you please ring her tomorrow – I've written down her number here. And there was another call from Lady Cynthia Musgrave who said she was your mother, Melpomene, but she said it wasn't urgent, she just wanted a chat. Is your mother really a Lady?"

Winnie looked quite awed!

"Thanks very much for those," said Mel, "yes, my Mama is a lady, and my late father was a Lord – but I am quite ordinary as you will find!"

"That all depends on how you judge it!" muttered Alex.

It was decided that all the business could wait for the next day. Mel telephoned home to see what arrangements Mrs M had made for dinner, and was told that she could whip something up in half an hour, but hadn't done so yet. So they decided to eat out, "And, Winnie, since it's your first day, you are invited too – do you like Italian food? And you can tell us all about yourself and your family, if you are willing!"

"Oh, Melpomene and Alex – I think I'm going to like this job, and I hope I can stay with the firm for a long time!"

"We'll see what we can do, Winnie," said Alex, "as I said before, I've got a couple of ideas in that direction, and one of them concerns Inspector Stephanie Walters, who you spoke with today."

Chapter 18

They all had a nice chat at the dinner – Mel and Alex told about their university specialties yet again, and Winnie said that before going to Pitman's College she had been apprenticed to a hairdresser for a while, but hadn't liked being patronized by some of the middle-class clientele, saying, "The higher in society they get, the nicer they are, generally – it's the ones who are unsure of themselves who are the snobbiest! The senior hairdressers can mostly find ways of coping with this, but I wasn't there long enough!"

She also told them about her flat-mates, "Dottie works in a travel agency – that's a nice job, but it's hard to get into – and Maureen is a student of photography at the Regent Street Polytechnic – she's got one of those tiny little German cameras you can put in your handbag – she won it in a national competition – you should see some of her pictures!"

Alex said, "You must introduce us to her, Winnie, we might be able to put some jobs her way!"

After the meal, Alex drove her back to her flat, saying "See you in the morning, Winnie – then you can tell me more about the person with the troublesome neighbour, before I call him back."

First thing after breakfast, Melpomene telephoned her mother, and found that indeed all she wanted to do was chat and catch up with developments at Crabbe and Crabbe. Mel said, "We can't tell you much about our current job, Mama, it is a bit sensitive – but there hasn't been any violence so far, cross fingers, and we'll let you know what we can, when we can – anyway, I can say that it concerns the fine art trade. Look after yourself, we might come and visit you again well before Christmas, with any luck!"

Then Alex said, "Let's drive to the office and dispose of Jimmy Manley's call next – I have a question for him anyway."

Winnie got the number and found Jimmy in, so Alex opened by saying, "Before I forget, Jimmy, can you look up a couple of car numbers for me? Here they are."

Jimmy said, "Right, I've got them. I'll ask Cec Thompson to get onto the car registry people with those – any more chores for us before we can exchange our other news?"

Said Alex, "Sorry to take advantage of you, Jimmy – all I can tell you about our current case is that it is about art dealers and could involve other countries."

"Not to worry, Alex, I know that things can get a bit sensitive from time to time – there are things that I won't even share with my close colleagues until they're sorted. I just wanted to let you know that a few more loose ends have been tidied up from your previous big case – it looks as though all the major villains will be safely put away – or hanged! – before the year is out! And it was good to have made contact with the Huddersfield police – it's so much easier to collaborate when you know someone!"

"And, Jimmy, we're working with the Northampton Constabulary, or will be shortly – have you ever come across a female DI called Stephanie Walters?"

"Can't say I have, Alex, are you saying I might, soon?"

"Who knows? So far, Jimmy, she is only a name to us, but we're going to telephone her right after we've talked to you. Good to hear from you that you're still in business. See you later – unless you have anything else to tell us today?"

"Only those car numbers, Alex – thanks, Cec – The first one is held by a car-hire firm in Reading, 'Robinson's Hire Cars and Hearses', and the other one is registered to a Mr William Satterfield."

"The devil it is!" exclaimed Alex, "That name again! But at least we know where Satterfield himself is at the moment – in jail in Reading, awaiting trial for running an illegal auction ring, thanks to a certain Melpomene Crabbe! We'll tell you the whole story later, Jimmy – you certainly deserve a proper account!"

"Are you sure he's in jail?" asked Jimmy, "and not out on bail? That sounds like a magistrates' court charge to me, and they don't normally keep people banged up for those! Would you like me to find out? Was he arrested by the Reading police? Right oh, I'll check and ring you back. Meanwhile, do you want to take down Satterfield's address? It's in Wimbledon – Pengelly House, Fairford Avenue."

Alex was astonished once again, "We were stopped right outside that address yesterday ourselves, would you believe! I wonder if Satterfield was there too?"

Melpomene was fascinated by all that when Alex related it to her, "So let's get onto DI Walters now and talk to her about the case, including these latest developments. I must say that, so far, all our police contacts have been remarkably helpful and valuable! So let's hope this situation continues! Can you try to get her, please, Winnie?"

She was not available when Winnie tried, but the man who answered said that she should have returned to the station within the hour, and he would ask her to ring back, if she had the number. Winnie assured him that she had, and also that there would be someone who could take the call.

Said Alex, "We need to talk about all this, and we can't possibly do that without tea and jam tarts! Can you oblige, Winnie, please?"

However, the conversation had hardly got started, though the tea and tarts were well under way, when the telephone rang. Alex picked it up, because he happened to be nearest, and it was Jimmy Manley, saying, "I guessed right, Alex, your Mr Satterfield was released on his own recognizance in the sum of four thousand pounds, reporting to the police weekly, for mention in three weeks' time at Reading Magistrates' Court. This means, of course, that he can get up to whatever shenanigans he wishes in the meantime! I often feel that the bail system in this country is designed for honest people only!"

No sooner had Jimmy and Alex finished their conversation than the telephone rang again. This time Winnie picked it up, then said to Melpomene, "It's Inspector Stephanie Walters."

Melpomene said, "Sorry we missed your call yesterday, Inspector. We asked your Chief Superintendent to recommend a bright young detective to us, and he picked you! We have a group of suspicious individuals in the Northampton area that we need some professional help with, if you are willing. We are trying to track down some activities connected with the fine arts, including a bunch we caught running an auction ring in the Bedford area, and others attempting to drive down the price of a painting by questioning its authenticity. Would you be interested in getting involved in these sorts of things, in particular checking out the latter group?"

Stephanie Walters seemed to be quite keen, "If it offers me a chance to get away from investigating rapes and domestic affrays, I'm your woman!"

Chapter 19

"Very good! I suppose that's one of the hazards of being a woman in a male-dominated environment!" said Melpomene, "If I wanted to drive up and have a talk with you – we'd probably need an hour or more – when would be a good time? Is it easy to find your station? I've only been to Northampton once before."

"I have my office in the main police station in Campbell Street, close to the city centre – anyone would direct you. I'll leave word that you can park in the police yard – what car do you drive?"

"Nothing very conspicuous!" said Mel, "Just a bright red Alvis two-seater! Do you need the number?"

"No, that description should be enough to identify it!" said Stephanie, "How about tomorrow afternoon – is that too soon for you?"

"Not at all, that will be excellent – I look forward to seeing you then!"

When Melpomene had rung off, she turned to Alex, saying, "I wonder if Jens-Olle would be willing to have Stephanie contact his post-graduate student colleague in Copenhagen – we already raised the possibility. It would be good if they could pool their expertise, since it seems to me that they will both be conducting similar searches. Shall I telephone him?"

"Why not?" said Alex, "Winnie, have you got a number in your book for Jens-Olle Pedersen when he's in London?"

"Let me see – yes, here we are. Shall I ring him now?"

Jens-Olle answered almost immediately and spoke to Melpomene, "Have you got a new secretary, Mel? That didn't sound like Marjorie."

Mel explained and Jens-Olle expressed his sympathy and hoped Marjorie would soon be up and around, then asked, "What was it you wanted to speak to me about, Melpomene? Something work-related, I hope! I have been discussing bureaucratic matters all morning, and that gets very boring!"

Mel explained about Stephanie Walters, and he said that so long as Mel passed on only the contact details for his assistant, that would be all right. "I have already impressed upon young Niels Mortensen the necessity for discretion, and so long as you can convince your Inspector Walters of the same, I think we shall be safe. If the names of any of the principals, like myself and Hugo, never get mentioned, no outsider will be able to penetrate our organization very deeply. And it may not have escaped you, Mel, that I have myself given you no other names than mine and Hugo's, which in any case you knew already! I'll give you Niels' details, are you ready to write them down?"

"Very satisfactory!" said Mel, after she had thanked him and put the receiver down, "I shall probably drop into the Hendersons' on the way, if I find I have enough time. Maybe I shall get a chance to talk to Arnold Henderson himself, but I'm not going to make a big thing of it if I miss him – Mildred has certainly got her wits about her – we shall see!"

She said to Winnie, "I won't take you to Northampton with me tomorrow, because we can't do without you here, but when Marjorie is back, how would you like to help Stephanie there while she's working on our case? If I know anything, they won't have any police clerks to spare on what might become a time-consuming job. The business will cover your share of the rent of your flat here, as well as your expenses in Northampton, of course."

Winnie looked very enthusiastic about the prospect and looked very close to coming over and kissing Melpomene!

Mel went on, "Now, what else did we line up to do today? Oh, I'll phone Marjorie and see how she is, first."

Marjorie sounded very cheerful and said she would be back at work in a day or two, "The doctor says it will be all right, but Mum is more cautious, bless her! Did you find a new girl?"

"Yes we did," Mel answered, "she's called Winnie, and you will meet her soon! But don't worry, she is not going to take your place – you are indispensible – we've got other plans for her. Look after yourself, and we'll see you in the office, but only when you are feeling a hundred per cent!"

"Now we should get in touch with that prospective client with the neighbour problems," said Alex, "Winnie, can you read us the notes you made, please?"

59

"Here we are, Alex, his name is Arthur Ralston, he lives in Hackney, and he didn't say exactly what his problem was with his next-door neighbour, just that he was at his wits' end! Shall I get him on the telephone?"

"In a moment, Winnie, I want to have a word with Mel first. What I'm wondering, Mel, is why he should think that a detective agency, rather than the police or the Council, could help him with a domestic problem?"

"Well, there's one way to find out, my darling, isn't there? Get Alex the number, Winnie, please!"

A woman answered and then said that her husband was at work, but could be reached by telephone, as he had his own office in his importing firm. She gave Winnie his direct number.

On the next attempt, Winnie spoke to Mr Ralston and told him that Alex Crabbe was calling.

"Good of you to call back, Mr Crabbe," he said when Alex introduced himself, "I gather you were out of the office when I rang before. It's rather a complicated situation I have at home, would it be possible for you to come to my place of work, or should I come to your agency – I have a quantity of correspondence I should like you to see."

"Tell me the address, and I will visit you, Mr Ralston, I need to get out from time to time!"

Alex hung up, saying, "I'm a bit curious about what this man imports, Melpomene, and whether he is an employee or the proprietor. I can find out these things more naturally at his premises than here without appearing too nosy."

Alex drove the Alvis to the address he had been given, finding that it was a Victorian-era factory building with a faint but still decipherable name over the front door that read, 'Wilshaw and Sons: Hides and Tallow'. He parked on the street and went up a couple of steps and in at the front door. There was an enquiries window, with a be-whiskered man reading a pink racing newspaper.

"Where will I find Mr Ralston?" Alex asked. The man said nothing, his eyes still on his paper, but rang a bell on the counter, whereupon a little girl of about ten or eleven emerged from a door by the side of the window. The man finally spoke, "Take this gentleman to see your father, Effie."

Chapter 20

Effie said nicely, "Please follow me, Sir," and headed off towards a lift at the end of the entrance hall. "we haven't had this lift very long, but Daddy lets me work it – it's really very easy. Please step in, and I will press the button that closes the door, and then I shall take you to the second floor where my Daddy's office is – you will see how it all works!"

At the second floor, Effie led him to a door that bore the name, 'Mr A. T. Ralston: General Manager.' She held it open and then left with a smile. Inside was an ante-room, where a grim-looking young woman with bobbed hair looked enquiringly at Alex without speaking.

Alex said "Alexander Crabbe – I have an appointment with Mr Ralston." Then the woman smiled and said, "Oh yes, I'll let him know you're here, please take a seat," and vanished into an inner office. She spoke to Mr Ralston and then ushered Alex in.

Arthur Ralston was younger than Alex had expected, maybe in his thirties, working in his shirtsleeves and taking a pencil from his mouth as he extended his hand, "Very good of you to come, Mr Crabbe! Did you have any difficulty finding us?"

"Not at all, and then a charming young person brought me to your office!"

"Ah yes, Effie – the apple of my eye! She is off school for a few days, partially because of the trouble that prompted my approach to your firm. Please take a seat, and I will try to explain. It is all rather complicated!"

"Do you mind me taking notes?" Alex asked, "Not at all," said Ralston, "later I will give you copies of some correspondence as well."

"This all started nearly two years ago. My poor wife had passed away after a long illness, and Effie and I thought it better to move away from the house and gardens that held so many of our fond memories. We found a modest little place in Hackney, which was quite a change, but Effie's school was still accessible by way of a short bus trip. She hadn't wanted to leave her friends, of course. Would you like a cup of tea or coffee? This narrative could take quite a while!"

"Thank you, that is very good of you, please continue, Mr Ralston. May I be rude and interpose a question at this point? I thought we spoke to your wife earlier today – were we mistaken?"

"Call me Arthur, please. The woman you spoke to is my housekeeper, Mrs Daventry – she is quite efficient at housework, but I fear she is delusional and has begun to think we are married! I will continue, if I may, and later everything will become much clearer, I hope. When we moved in, I thought it proper to introduce myself to the immediate neighbours. An unattached man with a young daughter might otherwise have prompted idle speculation! On one side I found a middle-aged couple, the Burkes – Dot and Alan, who were very friendly – we are on popping-in terms now! The other neighbour, Mr Considine, is quite a contrast – he hasn't even unbent enough to tell me his first name yet! He was not exactly rude when I approached him, but hardly welcoming, either. Little did I imagine then that he would present a serious problem later! More tea, Mr Crabbe?"

"No thanks, Arthur, call me Alex, please. So what happened next?"

"Yes, I realise I am stringing it out rather. I will get to the point immediately. About ten days ago, I was sitting reading my paper one evening, when the doorbell rang. Effie went to answer it – Mrs Daventry just comes in daily – and brought in Mr Considine, then left us and went to her room, I suppose. Considine said something I did not quite catch, so I asked him to repeat it, when he said 'nice girl, your daughter, looks good in her swimming costume!' As you might imagine, Alex, this upset me, so I'm afraid I snapped back, saying I didn't want him gawping at her, or something of the sort!"

"Did he react to this?"

"He certainly did! I can recall his words exactly! 'You'd better keep her on a shorter rein, Mr Ralston, or something bad might happen to her! I was going to put a business proposition to you, but now I'm not so sure!', and he got up to leave. Foolishly, as I now realise, I felt I had to mollify the man, so I said 'I'm a bit tired, forgive me!' or something of the sort, and he sat down again. My head was spinning, somewhat!"

"I can well imagine!" said Alex, "Did he put his proposition to you then?"

"If you can call it a proposition – I would have said more of a threat! He went on to say that he knew I was an importer, dealing in a range of household goods from continental manufacturers, and that he had information I was not declaring many of my transactions to HM Customs. He said that if I agreed to include some packages for him, he would make it worth my while and not inform the authorities – otherwise I might find myself up for substantial fines or even a jail sentence!"

"And were you doing what he accused you of – you can depend on my discretion, as though I were your solicitor – I am a solicitor, by the way!"

"So far as I am aware I have not condoned nor am doing any such thing – but I must say I have become suspicious that some of my employees or agents might be involved in misdoing! This is another reason that I turned to your firm, Alex!"

"You said you had some correspondence, too, Arthur – what was that about?"

Ralston pulled open a desk drawer and took out a pile of papers. "Here is the first, Alex, from Considine himself, from an address in Limehouse, not the next-door house. I got this the day after his visit here, I won't read it all, but you are welcome to take it away with you. It repeats his 'proposition' but adds something not mentioned before, 'I am speaking for my principal, who is a very powerful figure in cross-channel illicit trade. He confirms that I have his authority to make the offer, and if you agree, he will make arrangements to see you face-to-face, either in London or Le Havre.' The next letter complains that I have failed to respond to his offer, although four days have elapsed, and that the patience of his principal will soon be exhausted. The third letter repeats his implied threat, saying that if I do not wish to work with them, I must expect the consequences."

"Don't despair yet, Arthur!" said Alex, "There is something I would like you to do, and something encouraging to tell you. First of all, tell Considine to his face, as convincingly as possible, that you will meet with his principal in Le Havre. But don't commit anything to writing. Secondly, I am going to talk to a senior official I know in the French establishment, and suggest to him that he arrange a trap to be sprung at your meeting. You, of course, will not be the target, but the bait!"

Chapter 21

When Alex got back to the office he thought it was too late by that time to contact Jens-Olle to get Hugo's number, but decided that anyway he needed to discuss his plans thoroughly with Melpomene.

"What I wanted to check with you particularly," he said, "is whether it is wise to leave Arthur Ralston to meet this master smuggler on his own. He is – or I hope he is! – not used to dealing with devious criminals and might not be able to improvise if the meeting doesn't go as expected. Do you think one of us should accompany him as a minder?"

"I do see what you mean," said Mel, "but how would we explain our presence? And it could very well make the villain so suspicious he would call the meeting off. Another possibility would be for you to pretend to be Ralston and go in his place. But this is just as fraught – you don't know enough about his business or indeed about the import trade in general to be convincing. This crook hasn't risen to the top of his occupation by being naïve!"

"I have only put the idea to Ralston in the most general terms," said Alex, "and he needs a great deal more briefing before he sets out – and we don't even know whether Considine will go ahead and arrange the meeting – he could have second thoughts!"

Mel said, "We should raise all these points when we talk to Hugo Palance, if we can get in touch with him tomorrow. He may well have much better ideas! Anyway, it's time to go home now – I have checked with Mrs M and she is giving us roast pork with 'all the trimmins' tonight. Then we'll sleep on it and try to contact Hugo in the morning. Good night, Winnie – don't stay too long!"

"I won't!" said Winnie, "but I'm halfway though reading the file notes for your last couple of cases – they are almost better entertainment than Agatha Christie, though I must admit to a soft spot for Hercule Poirot – I've just finished 'The Murder of Roger Ackroyd' – there was a long waiting list for it at the library! See you in the morning, Mel and Alex."

When they arrived at the office the next day, there was Marjorie waiting for them! She had small plasters on some of her fingers, but said that she had tried typing at home and she was fine with it. She and Winnie had already become friends, and they had rearranged the outer office so there were places for each of them.

After a lot of hugging and kissing, Marjorie said, "If the firm could spring to it, we could do with a second typewriter, and a proper typist's chair to go with it, if there are going to be two of us permanently!"

"A good idea!" said Alex, "Perhaps you two could go on an expedition to pick them out, as you are the ones who know all about these things. I'll even give you a couple of signed cheques, if you promise not to decamp with all the firm's money!"

"It would be a bold thief who tried that on with a couple of detectives like you two!" said Winnie.

"Have there been any calls yet, this morning?" asked Mel, "I don't suppose the postman's been yet."

"No on both counts," said Marjorie, "but Winnie says you want to get in touch with Hugo Palance. What she didn't know is that his number, when he's in London, is already in the book – she assumed that we didn't have it, since you were talking about asking Jens-Olle Pedersen for it. Shall I try to get him for you?"

"Oh, yes please, Marjorie – I'll take it in the back office. Are you coming, Alex?"

Hugo replied straight away, and greeted Melpomene with obvious delight. And when he heard what was being planned, he fell in with it enthusiastically.

"I have no idea who he might be, this *voyou*! I will put one of my best agents on to this, and perhaps I will keep observation from a hidden position. Of course, I shall have some *gens robustes* waiting in the wings in case of trouble! Let me know immediately this *rendez-vous* has been set up, and we shall spring into action. I shall be available at this number until this evening, when I shall return to Paris. I will tell your secretary both my official number and my number at home – I do not usually give that out, but I am becoming quite excited!"

"We shall let you know the moment we know ourselves!" said Mel, "Alex is about to telephone Ralston to see whether he was able to talk to Considine last night. Thanks for being so enthusiastic about our mad plan! Here is Marjorie to take down the numbers."

As it was within business hours, and Alex didn't particularly wish to talk to the delusional Mrs Daventry, he rang Ralston's office. His secretary put him through straight away, as though she had been primed to do so.

"Hello, Alex," said Ralston, "Considine came round again last night, and I told him I was willing to meet his chief. He knew what cross-channel freight service I normally use, and that they sail twice a week, so he said I should travel over on the Thursday morning sailing next – that is the day after tomorrow, and go to a certain café near the docks as soon as I had disembarked. I should wear a white necktie and carry a Gladstone bag. He would contact me as soon as he had made sure I wasn't accompanied by anyone."

Alex said, "Go on Arthur, I'm getting this all down in shorthand – I was taught it at Law school. I think our opponents might have made a tactical error in choosing the meeting place. My contact can easily arrange to have scruffy-looking wharf labourers, or other unremarkable people keeping watch. What is the name of this café?"

"Unimaginatively, 'La Petite Café du Port' – there is also a 'Grande Café' I suppose. My French is not too bad, so I shall simply ask for directions."

"Thanks, Arthur, I shall pass this all on to my colleague in France. What time on Thursday will the ship dock?"

"The schedule says 11.15 am, but it all depends on how quickly the cargo was taken on, the weather and so on. Your people will no doubt allow plenty of margin each way, but you might mention it, for safety's sake! I am not so much concerned about the meeting itself, but I must say I am a little worried at leaving Effie at home, given Considine's doubtful remarks – what if he intends to hold her hostage? I shall have to set out for the docks quite early to catch the boat, before she goes to school!"

"Will she be going to school her usual way? She goes by bus, doesn't she? Melpomene or I, or both of us, will come to your house the night before to take care of her, so don't fret!"

Chapter 22

Ralston said, "That will make me feel a lot happier. Effie usually comes home by bus, walking the last couple of streets, and arriving about 4.30 or 5.00. Mrs Daventry doesn't finish until 6.30, but often I'm not home until 7 o'clock, so Effie is used to being on her own at home for a while. She usually does her homework then. So if you and your partner can arrange to come here before, say, 5 o'clock, we have her covered one way or another. You haven't been to our home, have you?"

"No, but we know the address," said Alex, "we shouldn't have any difficulty getting there by that time, it's not far. Effie has met me, of course. Melpomene is coming with me, so we look forward to seeing you tomorrow evening. We'll have a thorough briefing about the meeting then, so it will be fresh in your mind."

After Alex rang off, Melpomene said, "You seem to be a bit concerned about Effie, Alex. What sort of a kid is she?"

"She could be your younger sister, Mel – she is bright, enterprising, self-assured and possibly adventurous – but she's only ten or eleven, after all, so could be susceptible to suggestions. This neighbour of theirs, Considine, who is doing all the arranging for his boss, seems to be a thoroughly unsavoury character. When Arthur Ralston was telling me about him at the warehouse, I could see he was highly suspicious. Part of it could be his concern for Effie – she seems to be the centre of his life since he lost his wife."

"I can understand that!" said Mel, "I look forward to meeting Effie! Now, what preparations do we need to make before we travel to the wilds of Hackney tomorrow?"

"Well, the most important is to tell Hugo Palance about the arrangements. I hope he is still where we telephoned him earlier! Please try that number, Marjorie!"

Thankfully, Hugo picked up the telephone after only one ring – Alex thought he might have been sitting with his hand over the instrument.

"I have just been speaking to Arthur Ralston, Hugo," he said, and proceeded to relate all the details, to which Hugo grunted approvingly.

"I actually know Le Havre quite well, but the name of that café doesn't ring any bells with me – but there would have been no point in giving Ralston a false name. I will make the arrangements as soon as we finish this call – rely on me, I shall fix that place up like a rat-trap! And I shall also have some people loitering in the street outside. All armed, I should say – if these gentlemen are associated with others we have encountered lately, they will be desperate types! By the way, I believe you have my Paris number, I shall be taking the overnight ferry from Dover to Calais this evening."

"We'll keep our fingers crossed, Hugo – meanwhile we have some preparations to do on this side of the channel!"

"Now," said Melpomene, "I shall telephone Jimmy Manley! I have been meaning to ask him to check out this Considine since his name first arose!"

She was soon talking to DS Manley, "We were getting concerned about our favourite Detective-Sergeant, since we know you are getting bored there, Jimmy, with nothing to do but arrest a few sneak-thieves, so here is somebody more interesting! I'll give you his details first, and then put you into the picture a bit more! He is called Considine, first name unknown, and he lives in Hackney, which must be quite close to you at Mile End Road. Here is his address, do you want to write it down? – He lives next door to our latest client, Arthur Ralston, who is at number 16, and he has attempted to involve him in a plot to cheat HM Customs. All the action is about to happen in Le Havre, which is why we haven't got onto you before now, but it could possibly link into all this illicit art business we're investigating."

Melpomene then related the whole story to an appreciative Jimmy.

"Right you are, Mel!" said Jimmy, "DC Thompson is itching to get on his bike again – aren't you, Cec? – so he'll look through our files and records and then pay Mr Considine a visit, perhaps, unless you've got him up to something else?"

"We shall be at Mr Ralston's house early tomorrow afternoon, Jimmy, so if Cec wants to call in, we'll have a yarn with him."

Then Melpomene exclaimed, "I nearly forgot! How long will it take me to get to Northampton? It's already 1.30, and I told Stephanie Walters I would be with her this afternoon!"

"Don't panic, Mel!" said Alex, "I don't think it will take you more than a couple of hours, so it will still be afternoon! Don't speed, though. Meanwhile I'll phone her and say you could possibly be a little late, all right?"

"Thanks, my darling! Off I go, then – Campbell Street Northampton, here I come!"

In the event, Melpomene reached the Northampton Police station just before four o'clock. She drove up to the gates of the yard and a young constable came up and said. "Mrs Crabbe? You can park over there, next to that Humber. DI Walters is waiting for you in her office. Go in that door, turn right, and you'll see a door with 'CI Branch' on it." He saluted smartly.

Mel found the office with no difficulty, rapped on the door and went in. A tall woman, her black hair in a shining bob, was conferring with a colleague, standing by his desk. They were both in plain clothes, if you could call Stephanie's outfit 'plain'! She was wearing a tailored suit, which Melpomene recognised as a Burberry, over a frilled scarlet silk blouse, with sheer taupe silk stockings and high-heeled shoes to suit. She straightened up as she saw Mel, and ushered her into her office.

"I saw you looking at my outfit!" she said, "Nice, yes? I had to go to a company board meeting this morning – we're investigating some dubious share dealings – so my normal dowdy clothes might have made me conspicuous – I was playing the role of an executive from a competing firm! I can't bear to take them back to the shop just yet!"

"Nor would I, in your position!" said Mel, "It makes me think that it's about time I bought myself some more outfits! But, to business! Since we talked, I have made arrangements for you to work with a Danish policeman *cum* student on tracking down some of the members of these gangs dealing with art objects in various nefarious ways – forging, smuggling, stealing and so on. We have an exercise coming up in France tomorrow, against an attempt to induce an honest importer to infiltrate smuggled goods into his shipments from the continent into Britain."

"So the men whose names you passed me are also involved?"

"So we think – this whole organization has many arms, we believe, and so all we can do is nibble away at the edges until we can get a handle on the big boys running it. And we have to be prepared for them to react in devious and vicious ways!"

Chapter 23

"We know very well," said Melpomene, "that what we are asking you to do falls outside your normal police duties to some extent, so as some compensation, we have arranged for one of our staff to act as an assistant for you – to be paid by our agency, of course. I am most impressed with her, her name is Winnie Morris and she is an expert Pitman-trained typist and has a good mind. We are hoping that you will be able to accept this offer – what do you say?"

"This sounds very good to me – when can she start?"

"We first need to find somewhere for her to stay – perhaps you can recommend an estate agency here who deals in flat rentals? Crabbe and Crabbe will pay the rent, and we are paying her share of the flat she normally occupies in London."

"No need to look for a place!" said Stephanie, "As long as we get on with one another, she can stay with me. I have a small house left to me by my parents, and I have been letting out one room on a casual basis. I have no tenant at the moment, so your Winnie will be very welcome. Crabbe and Crabbe can pay me what I have been charging my previous tenants, and Winnie and I can share the housekeeping expenses, if she is willing."

"Wonderful!" said Mel, "She can work from your place, or at the station, whichever suits best. We're buying her a new typewriter, so she will need a table or desk for it."

"No problem! We can discuss our best way of working once she's here – will that be all right? I have a few questions for you before you go – perhaps you can stay for a meal with me and we can talk over the table?"

"That sounds lovely, I'll telephone Alex and let him know where I've got to! But I've had another thought, I'll also ring Mildred Henderson and see whether she would give us a few minutes, if you are willing to come and be introduced to her. The sooner you two meet, the better, since she knows many of the people we think are conspirators already."

Mildred was happy to hear from Mel, and said that Arnold was at home and was also keen to meet her and her friend – would 8 o'clock be acceptable? This was fine with Stephanie, "If you don't mind me reheating a casserole from last night – they often taste better the second day!"

"I didn't mention to Mildred that you were a police inspector, Stephanie – are you happy with that? I thought it might inhibit what they say if they knew that." Stephanie didn't mind, "She will never suspect that a humble copper would wear this outfit – I'm certainly not going to change out of it now!"

Stephanie's casserole was indeed delicious. While it was heating, Mel had been taken on a tour of the house and shown the room that Winnie might occupy. It reminded Melpomene of the college room she had occupied at LSE, with a bed-settee, a desk and chair, a wardrobe and a tallboy. "She'll have to share the bathroom and lavatory with me," said Stephanie, "but this has always worked out fine before, even with male lodgers. We two women just won't have to be as careful about keeping doors closed!"

Melpomene had to refresh her memory about the Henderson's address, but Stephanie was familiar with the district, so they rolled up in the Alvis right on time. In Mildred's sitting room the two women were introduced to Arnold, who welcomed them warmly. He was a little different from the mental picture that Mel had – quite tall and with thick dark hair – and was very affable.

"Have you had any success with your investigation?" he asked, "The last I heard was that you were trying to track down Postlethwaite, Satterfield and the others – anything more recently?"

"We have an address for your William Satterfield," said Melpomene, "so the hunt continues – we will let you know when and if he turns up! You will probably also be interested that we caught a Keith Satterfield running an illegal auction ring and he will be charged with that soon!" she continued, "Either he is flexible about his first name or we have bagged a relative, since Satterfield is not a common name – but I suppose it's still possible that the two are not connected. Unfortunately for us, Keith has been released on bail and seems to have gone to ground!"

"It sounds as though you are being kept busy!" said Henderson, "You may be interested to hear that I brought in an independent expert – the curator of the Northampton Museum and Art Gallery – to have a look at my Daphnis and Chloe, and after meticulous examination he told me that he is absolutely certain that it is genuine and has not been interfered with! I rang Severin DuPlessis earlier today and told him this, and apologized for doubting him and his conservator, Miss Mainwaring. So I hope that DuPlessis will consider that case closed."

"Yes, I hope so too!" said Melpomene, "But the fact remains that the police are still interested in Mr Postlethwaite, because his accusation has caused a great deal of commotion and was apparently made with malicious intent. Slander can be a criminal offence and this whole incident amounts to slander against Mr DuPlessis and his gallery."

"If not criminal slander," added Stephanie, "it could be regarded as malicious falsehood, which is a tort in law, as any lawyer could verify."

"We shall ask Alex about that," said Melpomene, "one way or another, Postlethwaite has sinned, and this requires retribution. But we need to find him first!"

Mildred Henderson said, "I'm afraid I am a poor hostess – can I offer you any refreshment? I understand you have had dinner, but how about a liqueur?"

"Thank you so much!" said Melpomene, "but I should get Stephanie back home – we have both had a busy day! I introduced you both to Stephanie, because she will be pursuing enquiries for us, here in Northampton and in the region."

"I will be in touch!" said Stephanie, and they both shook hands with the Hendersons and went back to the Alvis.

"You must stay the night," said Stephanie, "we can't have you driving back to London at this hour! We can telephone Alex as soon as we get to my house."

Melpomene gratefully fell in with this suggestion, had some chocolate and a bath, borrowed a suit of pyjamas from Stephanie and said, "I will now test the bed-settee for Winifred!"

So she did, and the test was so satisfactory that Stephanie had a job waking her in the morning.

After breakfast, the two hugged and Melpomene set off for London feeling quite pleased with the visit. She drove straight to the office and immediately demanded tea and jam tarts.

Chapter 24

"We've eaten all the tarts already!" said Winnie, "Only kidding! I'll put the kettle on straight away. We just had a call from your Mr Ralston at Tilbury docks, who was about to board the 'Alicia Budworth' for Le Havre. Alex wrote down some notes, but he's on the telephone again right now. How was your trip?"

"Very good, Winnie, and you'll be particularly pleased, too! I'll tell you and Marjorie and Alex all about it once he's hung up."

Alex explained that he had been talking to Hugo and letting him know that Arthur Ralston was on his way to Le Havre, complete with white necktie and a Gladstone bag that he had borrowed from someone at work.

"It's up to Commissaire Palance and his men, now!" said Alex, "I'm fairly confident, but I shan't really be able to settle until I hear how it all went off. If he can get to a telephone, Ralston will call us at his house as soon as he has anything to report, and Hugo will telephone the office here."

"Did he say anything about Effie?" asked Melpomene.

"Only that he hadn't told her any more than that he was off on a business trip and that Mel and I would be coming to the house in the afternoon. She was still at home when he left, and Mrs Daventry was already there, so Effie will walk to her bus stop at her usual time. She's probably at school by now. How was Northampton?"

"It was a very successful visit," said Mel, "I think we have done very well with Stephanie Walters – as they say in the trade, she has a mind like a steel trap! She was very pleased to hear that Winnie will be her assistant, and she has even offered her spare room for her, if she would like. I can vouch for the comfort of the sofa-bed she has for you, Winnie – I slept on it very soundly last night! We must get a new typewriter for you quickly, so you can get familiar with it before you go. I must say I have mixed feelings about losing you so soon! But with any luck, you and Stephanie will be able to clear up all this business quickly so you can return here!"

"Did you get to see Mildred Henderson?" asked Alex.

"Yes and her husband, too! I was pleasantly surprised, he is quite nice! And he had brought in his own art expert, who convinced him the 'Daphnis and Chloe' is truly the genuine article. He has already spoken to Severin DuPlessis and told him he is in the clear! And Stephanie has been introduced to the Hendersons, which will help in the chase after Postlethwaite and Co. By the way, I have only just woken up to the fact that there are two Satterfields – Keith, of the auction ring, and William, the one at the Henderson dinner party. We know from the car number plate that it is William who lives in Wimbledon, but as for Keith, we're puzzled."

Said Alex, "Of course, they could be the same person – or brothers – or father and son, for that matter. But all this speculation is a bit pointless until we find out a great deal more about the organization, if there is one at all!"

Then Melpomene said, "Alex and I need to have some lunch before we set off for darkest Hackney – I have had nothing this morning apart from two jam tarts and what they called a bacon butty in a lorry-drivers' place on the road from Northampton!"

"Winnie," said Alex, "have you got a preference for a new typewriter? Maybe you've had the use of various models in your previous jobs, or at Pitman's?"

"I do have a favourite, yes," replied Winnie, "but are you sure I should have the new one, perhaps Marjorie deserves one first! One that I really like is the Royal 10 – it is very quiet because it has felt on the bottom, so it would be good for me to use in Stephanie's house – the advanced students at Pitman's got to use those."

"I'm happy to stick with my faithful Underwood!" said Marjorie.

"Do you know who sells them?" asked Melpomene, "Perhaps you could phone up and order one to be delivered, if they will do it. I should think we could fit a typewriter in the dicky seat of the Alvis when it's time to go to Northampton."

"Why not try Selfridges, then – they should have them, they have everything else, nearly!" said Alex, "Can you look up the number, one of you typewriter experts, and give them a call! And if they have them in stock, and can deliver, find out the total price – we'll leave you a cheque, and you can just fill in the amount. But now we have to set out for Hackney, grabbing a bite on the way."

They were at the Ralston house by 2.30, parking a little way up the street, so their presence would not be obvious should Considine come visiting. Mrs Daventry let them in, saying, "I'm very sorry, but my husband must be at work, he left quite early this morning."

"But we've come to visit Mr Ralston, not your husband!" said Melpomene gently, which made the woman look quite confused, saying, "Of course, I knew that – you are from the office, aren't you?"

Mel didn't persist in explaining, thinking there was no point, and asked "When does Effie usually come home from school, Mrs Daventry?"

"Oh, the buses vary, and she can't always catch one straight away – sometimes it's four o'clock, but other times not until five. I'll make a pot of tea, shall I, while you wait. Do you want to listen to the wireless, they have nice music on at this time of day? There's the papers, too, we take the Times and a popular one. Effie has a comic, but it doesn't come today – I could fetch one from her room if you want."

Mel and Alex passed the time one way and another, until the peace was broken by the sound of someone running up the front path and Effie burst in the front door and slammed it behind her.

She was panting and agitated – Melpomene took her in her arms and she calmed down, "What was all that?" Mel asked "Are you all right now? Would you like a glass of water?"

"Oh, I'm so glad you are here!" said the little girl, "Please Mr Crabbe, look outside and see if anyone's there, and I'll tell you what happened!"

She sat down next to Mel on the settee and said, "It was like this. I got on my usual bus, and went upstairs – I like travelling on top, because you get a good view. When we got near to my stop, I stood up to leave and then I spotted Mr Considine waiting by the fence just past the stop! Daddy had told me I should be careful of him and not to speak to him at all, so seeing him there frightened me a bit, so I sat down again. I didn't think he had seen me, but when the bus started up again he began trotting after it, so he must have spotted me!"

Chapter 25

Effie went on, getting a little calmer now, "When I got off the bus, I looked back – the bus had just turned a corner and there was nobody in sight yet, so I started to run home along the road that turns into this street. After a bit, I got a stitch in my side, so I had to stop for a moment – and then I saw Mr Considine was only fifty yards behind me, so I made a final effort and got here just in time. He was about three houses away by then – luckily I had my key ready and you know the rest!"

Alex was looking out of the front window and said, "No signs of him now, Effie, maybe he's given up and gone away."

"But he lives next door, Mr Crabbe – he's probably gone indoors!"

"Tell you what," said Melpomene, "he doesn't know me, why don't I knock at his door and pretend to be an estate agent – I've played that role before, so I know my lines! Then I can get an idea of what he's doing, maybe, or at least what state of mind he's in. While I'm keeping him busy, Alex, you can ring Mile End Road and see if Jimmy can get some police here quickly to pick him up for questioning about the conspiracy. We know he's involved, you've seen the letters he wrote to Arthur Ralston!"

"Cec Thompson is supposed to be coming here anyway," said Alex, "maybe he's had a puncture or something! But it would be good to have greater numbers. I'll get on to Jimmy straight away. Meanwhile, take this, it's already loaded and cocked, you just have to slip the safety – but you know how to do this, don't you, my darling!" And Alex took his Luger from his shoulder-holster and passed it to Mel, who put it into her shoulder bag, next to some papers.

Effie's eyes, of course, were as big as saucers! Seeing this, Alex said, with a wink, to Mel, "Don't shoot him unless you really have to, Mel, remember all the paperwork you had to do last time!"

There was no immediate reaction when Melpomene rang Considine's front door bell, so she rang again and waited. The door was opened and he appeared, looking annoyed, "What is it? I've only been home five minutes and I'm being pestered!"

Mel smiled sweetly and said, "I'm sorry if it is inconvenient, Mr Considine, would you like me to come back another time? I only need a few minutes."

"Oh, go ahead, then!" he said, grumpily, "Make it snappy!"

"My name is Natalie Brookes," Mel said, "I'm from Preston and Wilberforce, estate agents in Hackney High Street – you probably know our offices, next to the Westminster Bank. We are trying to add to our listings, as we cannot keep up with the demand for property. We have many prospective buyers who are offering fantastic prices for houses in this district, so we can easily make some competing offers – or you might like to put the place up for auction. Only yesterday, I sold a house quite like this one for over a hundred pounds more than it cost new, four years ago. Could I step in for a moment and get a general impression of your house, please? I can see already that it is very nicely appointed and tastefully decorated."

"I haven't got time for all this!" said Considine, getting red in the face, "Go away – I never called you!"

Melpomene stood her ground, even stepping forward a little, trying to provoke him, but he simply pushed her out of the doorway. As she said to the others, later, "I had my hand on my gun, but thought better of it! If he had grabbed me, it might have been a different story! Did you get on to Jimmy Manley, Alex?"

"I did, and he is sending a car full of policemen. They should be here any time – it's less than two miles from the police station to here. Let me have my gun back again, please, and I'll keep watch in the back garden, in case he makes a dash for it when he sees them."

Alex found that the back gardens gave onto a narrow laneway, so he took up a position by the back fence where he could keep an eye on Considine's back gate without being obvious. He heard a car draw up and hammering on Considine's front door, with shouts of "Police! Open up!"

It went quiet then, and nobody emerged from the back door of the house, so Alex went back to rejoin the others, who by that time were standing on the front steps, watching the activities of the police. After only a few minutes, two of them led Considine out in handcuffs and bundled him into the back of the car. A sergeant came up to them, saying "Mr and Mrs Crabbe,

Sergeant Hancock, Mile End Road. DS Manley will call you later and fill you in. I gather this man will be charged with conspiracy to commit a felony, and you may be required to give evidence. Ah, look, here comes DC Thompson! Bicycle trouble, eh, Cec?"

"Yes, Sergeant, my chain came off!" he said, holding up his black greasy hands, "So I've missed all the fun, have I?"

The sergeant laughed, but kindly, "Never mind, Cec, there will be other days!"

Once the police car had driven off, Mel said to Cec Thompson. "You'd better come in and get that stuff off your hands! Are you ready for a cup of tea after all your efforts?"

She called to Mrs Daventry, who had been hovering in the background, her eyes nearly as wide as Effie's, saying. "Could you please make us some tea, Mrs Daventry, and have you any biscuits or cakes?"

Effie said, "I know we've got some coconut macaroons somewhere, would they be all right?"

While they were relaxing over the refreshments, the telephone rang and Effie ran to answer it, "Oh Daddy!" she said, "Are you safe and well? We dealt with Mr Considine just now, I'll tell you all about it, but tell me how you are first."

She listened for a moment and then passed the telephone to Alex, saying, "Daddy is fine and he wants to talk to you!"

Alex had a longish conversation with Arthur Ralston, finishing by saying, "That's excellent, Arthur, you must be feeling quite relieved! When will you be back? Do you want to speak with Effie again?"

He explained to the others, while Effie was on the telephone, that the trap had worked well, "He says that he was approached by a swarthy individual – he says he looked like the typical gangster from a Hollywood thriller – who told Arthur to follow him outside the café. When he refused, the crook drew a knife and waved it in his face with a stream of abuse, mostly in French. Then he was grabbed from behind by two big guys – one who Arthur had taken for a drunkard, slumped at a table, and the other who was dressed as a priest, in a long soutane with a biretta on his head, who had apparently been taking up a collection from the café patrons."

Chapter 26

Alex went on, "At that point in his story, Arthur said he would have another word with Effie, and then get back to us later, because he was calling from the police station, and the inspector there needed to interview him more extensively."

Melpomene was concerned about leaving Effie alone, or in the tender care of the delusional Mrs Daventry, which amounted to the same thing, so said quietly to Alex, "Leave me your pistol, and I'll stay here until Effie goes to school tomorrow, Considine is not the only member of this gang in the district, I should think." To which Alex replied, "Not a chance! I'll stay with you, my dear! So let's ring the office and let them know – they should still be there, it's not half past five yet – and we should tell Caroline and Mrs M, too."

When Marjorie answered, she said, "Oh, I'm glad everything went off all right. It's a good idea of yours to stay there, too, if I was a ten-year-old girl – or even a woman of my age – I should be quite anxious, knowing that there are those sorts of people around! But there's something else – the French gentleman, M. Palance is it? – called to say that he would like you to call him at his Paris number as soon as convenient – this was only half an hour ago, and I was going to telephone you, but you were engaged. I'll give you his number – but I suppose you have it in your little book already!"

Alex checked with Effie that she had finished speaking with her father, then asked the exchange for the Paris number. He was told that the cross-channel lines were all in use, but that they would call him back when one became free. As it happened this only took five minutes or so.

"Bonjour, Hugo!" said Alex, when Palance answered, "Do you want to talk to Melpomene, or will I do?"

"You will do!" was the reply, "I have some news which might be disappointing to both of you, I'm afraid. I'm devastated to have to admit that our French police service has blundered in this case, although they were rather forced into it. The *apache* who confronted M. Ralston in the café was interrogated, of course, and was found to be known to the Le Havre police as a very small fish. He was to have taken Ralston to the substantive meeting with his principal – whose name he would not divulge, or did not know – I suspect the latter. When Ralston understandably refused to cooperate, he threatened him with a knife and our people were forced to apprehend him. Had Mr Ralston kept his nerve and gone with this wretch, we might have had a chance to catch the big one! *C'est la vie, mon ami!* I was told this sorry tale by Inspecteur Fouchard of the Le Havre station, who has taken charge of the case. I instructed him to make sure that M Ralston is looked after until he is able to return to England, but I was not convinced that he would take this responsibility seriously – I believe he was resentful of him over the fumble at the café! So in a little while I will make further enquiries. Your Marjorie tells me you are at the Ralston house – will you be staying there? She gave me the number and I will call whenever there are further developments."

Alex relayed this to Mel, who said that it was a comfort that Hugo was in charge as she had great faith in him. She went to speak to Mrs Daventry, who was about to leave, to find out what there was in the house for an evening meal, which turned out to be not very much! She asked Effie whether there were any shops close by that would still be open.

Effie said, "I'm afraid not, at this hour, except for the fish and chip shop!"

"Well, fish and chips it will be!" said Mel, "I haven't had fish an chips wrapped in newspaper for ages. Tell Alex where it is, and he will take our orders and go and queue up! I will stay and mind the telephone. When you get back, Alex, use a secret knock and we'll know it's you and not a villain – three knocks, a space and then three more should do it. Does that sound OK, Effie?"

"Or he could just call out!" said the practical Effie.

Alex' expedition to the fish and chip shop was successful – they ate the meal off plates with knives and forks instead of straight from the newspaper wrapping – as a concession to civilization, as Melpomene said, even though it meant a certain amount of washing up.

They were all settling down to a game of cribbage when the telephone rang. Melpomene answered, and it was Hugo Palance again. "Is the child within earshot?" was his first question, "Yes," said Mel, "is there a problem?"

"I will tell you," said Hugo, "but you will have to be careful what you say in response because of the child – Arthur Ralston has been abducted! It happened because my stiff-necked *inspecteur de police* at Le Havre thought that it would be sufficient to lodge Ralston in a *pension* overnight, without taking any precautions to have it carefully watched! It appears that, while he was taking dinner with the host's family, a person dressed in a police uniform appeared at the door and asked for Ralston by name. When he went to see what was wanted, this so-called policeman and another man threw a coat or something over his head and rushed him to a waiting car. The landlord saw this happen but was too shocked to intervene – however he telephoned the police station immediately to enquire what it was all about, so raising a general alarm!"

Melpomene controlled the expression of astonishment that was her immediate reaction, and turned to Alex, saying, so that Hugo could hear, "Oh, Alex, there has been a procedural problem at Le Havre, and Hugo has to follow this up, so it may delay Arthur's return to London. I'll tell Hugo that we will take Effie back home with us – if she doesn't mind missing school tomorrow – then it will be the weekend. Did you hear all that, Hugo?"

"Well done, Melpomene!" said Hugo, "so I shall telephone you at your home or at your office, depending on the time of day, as soon as I have any news. Rely on me – I can call on better men than that foolish *inspecteur* – who will have to talk very hard if he is to avoid demotion! Good night for now!"

Mel hung up and turned to Effie, "Did you hear all that – will you be sorry to miss school tomorrow?"

"No, Mel, not at all!" was the child's answer, "I probably couldn't have concentrated on my lessons anyway. We should telephone Miss Huxstep, my teacher, in the morning and explain that it's not my idea!"

"Right then!" said Alex, "Go and pack some overnight things and a clean dress for tomorrow, Effie – have you got a small bag or suitcase? And you will need a warm coat and perhaps a scarf and a woolly hat – it can get chilly in the dicky seat of our Alvis at night, even though it isn't far! Will you help her, Mel?"

"If she needs help, yes!" It was less than half an hour later that they left a note for Mrs Daventry, shut up the house and set off for the flat.

Chapter 27

Caroline met them at the door and fussed over Effie as soon as she saw her, helping her off with her coat and hat and asking her if she was warm. "Oh yes, thank you! I really enjoyed the ride – I haven't been in such a super car before!"

"Would you all like something to eat?" asked Caroline, "I think Mrs M was working on some sort of pie earlier on, so let's see whether that's in a state to be served yet. Of course, it can be saved until tomorrow!"

"Just something small, please," said Alex, "we gorged ourselves on skate and chips an hour ago. But we could all do with tea, I should think. How about you, Effie, are you a tea drinker, or would you like chocolate?"

"Oh, chocolate, please!" said Effie, "Daddy never thinks of it at home! Can we play cribbage again, we had hardly started before?"

This suggestion was taken up and Caroline joined them in the game. Mrs M excused herself, saying, "Thanks all the same, but I'll get on with me knitting!"

Over breakfast, Melpomene asked Effie what she would like to do and she said she would like to go to the office if that was all right, as she had read about detectives but had not seen them at work. "Oh, yes you have!" said Mel, "What do you think all that was yesterday – isn't helping a fair damsel escape from a villain, who is then tricked into being arrested, close enough to detective work for you?"

Effie giggled and said, "I would still like to see your office, though!"

When they arrived, the first thing Winnie did, after introducing herself to Effie, was to show them all her brand-new Royal typewriter and demonstrate some sample typing.

"What we need now," she said, "is a stock of headed notepaper, so Marjorie and I don't have to type out the details every time. Would you like me to go and pick out a few samples, so we can get a few reams printed up?"

Then the telephone rang and Mel took the call in the back office while Effie was being shown how to use the new typewriter, but it was not Hugo as she had thought, but Stephanie Walters calling from Northampton Police Station.

"I just had a call from Niels Mortensen in Copenhagen," she said, "I didn't think you had given him my number, but he must have tracked me down – not a difficult task for someone in the trade who knew my name and where I work. Anyway, he sounded very keen to collaborate with us, as he had picked up tantalizingly few traces of the scent over there. He will actually come to Northampton in a few days – and I suppose I shall get the chance of a return visit to Denmark too, which should be very interesting."

"That sounds all very promising!" said Mel, "Have you had any success with your end of the hunt yet?"

"Actually, yes! I have found a connection between the elusive Satterfields – you guessed right, they are two brothers – and the man they call 'Fido' – whose real name is Henry Barker. Besides all having various occupations around Northampton, William Satterfield and Barker were suspected, two or three years ago, of being involved in a break-in at a mansion on the outskirts of town here during which several valuable etchings were stolen. There was insufficient evidence and no charges were laid. The eleven etchings, all small, no more than ten inches by eight, have never been recovered. They have been listed on the schedules of stolen goods that are circulated by the police to all galleries and antique shops, but haven't yet been picked up. My guess is that they have entered the 'grey market' and are being sold on to those dealers who are not too meticulous in checking their merchandise. There is a whole range of honesty in the world of art, objects of *vertu* and antiques, from the pure to the extremely dodgy, and it is extremely difficult to determine who is which. That makes the job very interesting to me, actually!"

"I suppose," said Melpomene, "that we shall bump into such illicit operators fairly often during our investigations! I would dearly like to have a chance to search the Wimbledon address we have been given for William Satterfield, especially as it seems to be the headquarters for the auction rings. By the way, when is Niels Mortensen coming to visit you? I would very much like to meet him, so please let me know as soon as the date is set. Meanwhile, are you ready to have Winnie Morris come and join you? She has her new typewriter and is itching to use it in earnest."

"Let's leave it until after the weekend, Melpomene, I'm entered for my club's tennis tournament on Saturday that might be the last for the year, so I don't want to miss it!"

"If you're a tennis player, Stephanie, you must come down to my family's hotel in Hampshire some time, maybe next Spring. Have some good matches and we'll talk to you on Monday!"

As Mel hung up the telephone, it rang again, and she heard the voice of Hugo Palance, slightly miffed by the sound of it, "Maybe you should consider getting a second line for your office, Melpomene! I've been trying to get through to you for at least twenty minutes."

"Oh, sorry, Hugo – I'll talk to Alex about arranging that. Your call is urgent, I gather?"

"It is, rather, but it's good news this time! Arthur has been liberated from durance vile! When the landlord of the pension from which he was abducted was questioned he recalled that the motor that the kidnappers were using looked like the standard Citroën *traction avant* that all our police have now – they will not be released, however, to the general public by the manufacturer until the contracts for the police fleets have been completely filled. So the movements of all the cars belonging to the district were checked and satisfactorily accounted for, except for the one assigned to *Inspecteur* Fouchard, which was not in its proper place in the headquarters garage! I instructed the *Commandant Divisionaire* to have Fouchard detained and questioned. To cut a long story short, the car was found in the garage of his private house, and a further search discovered Arthur Ralston in a cellar there – very peeved but none the worse for wear! Of course Fouchard and his driver are now under arrest! They have been sent to my separate unit at the *sûreté générale* so that our specialist interrogation team can determine what, if any, connections they have to the art underground, as we might start to call it."

"Congratulations Hugo!" said Mel, "Will Arthur be returning home soon? Can I tell Effie?"

"By all means tell her that her father will be coming home, probably by Sunday – but she need not be told he was confined by these crooks! If Arthur wants to tell her in his own good time, that is up to him – from what you have said, she is an extraordinarily robust little girl! By the way, Jens-Olle tells me that there are encouraging developments in Denmark, too!"

Chapter 28

Melpomene passed on the good news to the others, simply saying, for the moment, that Arthur Ralston would be coming home on Sunday, which made Effie clap her hands with delight, and that more villains had been apprehended. Mel also told Alex what Hugo had said about a second telephone line.

Alex replied, "He's right, of course! Could you look into what's needed, please, Marjorie? This is the spur we need to bring the rest of the office up to scratch, especially with our huge increase in staff! As Winnie and Marjorie have suggested, we need proper desks, typing chairs and so on – not to mention nice-looking headed stationery. And we should get rid of the old wooden filing cabinets – when you try to open the drawers, I've noticed they squeak, and stick quite often. To do all this modernizing, we can use the windfall we got from Winstanley Holdings as an *ex gratia* payment – I don't expect we'll get lump sums of that size very often!"

"But," said Marjorie, "our ordinary fees are coming in more promptly now – without needing to send in the heavy mob to break any arms – but I must admit that I've occasionally given some of the slow payers a bit of a verbal prod – very politely, of course!"

"It's over to you two, Marjorie and Winnie!" said Alex, "Come up with some plans and persuade Mel and me to spend the money. See what you can do before next Friday! Now I need another cup of tea!"

"You've been sitting there, taking it all in, Effie," said Melpomene, "but we'll have to find you something to do or you will get bored! What would you like to do?"

"Could I go to the telephone place with Marjorie, please and help her pick out new telephones? If you are going to get another line, you will need to change those, too. In my Daddy's work they have a private switchboard, with their own operator – that would be too much for Crabbe and Crabbe, I think – but I'm sure you could look at some of those new telephones with dials, so you don't have to ask the operator to get the number all the time! Daddy even lets me dial our home when we need to speak to Mrs Daventry. It's easy!"

Marjorie said, "It takes a member of the new generation to keep us up with the new developments! I hereby appoint you as my technical assistant, Effie – we shall go to the showroom first thing tomorrow, if they are open on Saturdays! Perhaps Alex can take us?"

Melpomene had been looking through the newspaper, and suddenly said, "Oh good, tomorrow night they are showing the award-winning movie, 'Wings' with Clara Bow, Buddy Rogers and Richard Arlen! Effie might enjoy that! – what do you say, Effie, it's all about fighter pilots in the War, mightn't it be too old for you?"

"I'd love to go!" said Effie, "It's Sunday the day after, so I can have a lie-in if it finishes too late!"

The doorbell rang and Winnie went to answer it. The others could hear that there was a short muttered conversation, and then Winnie brought in an elderly woman, well-dressed and nicely made-up. "This is the Countess Vibrovska," said Winnie, she would like to speak to one of our operatives – would one of you oblige?"

Mel stepped forward and took the woman's hand, "I am Melpomene Crabbe, Countess," she said, "would you like to come with me into the office? Then you can tell me your concern in private."

She invited the woman to take the only comfortable chair, making a mental note to herself that a better arrangement would be needed when the office was refurbished.

The woman said, with a shy smile, "I do not expect your secretary to be familiar with Polish spelling, but I should tell you that my name is spelt 'W,y,b,r,o,w,s,k,a', and that my first name is 'Dorota' – spelt as it sounds! What I have come to ask about concerns a dispute I am having over the leasing of property in Hampstead. I believe that the estate agent thinks that anyone with an accent must be easily duped! He is telling me all sorts of stories about leases, claiming that the landlord has the right to evict a tenant, such as myself, without having to show cause or give notice. This seems to me unworkable as well as unreasonable!"

"Excuse me, Countess, I should like to bring my partner, Alexander, in on this – he is a qualified solicitor, whereas I know little of the relevant laws."

Alex was introduced and listened to the Countess' story, and more details that she had not told Mel, with Alex asking pertinent questions throughout, up to the point where he asked, "Has the estate agent given you the landlord's name? And has he shown you the real property description?"

"No, neither!" said the Countess, "I thought this strange, but assumed it was simply English practice. The laws in Poland, I believe, are completely different."

"That is so," said Alex, "in England the basis is common law, supported by precedent, whereas many countries on the European continent rely on the Code Napoléon, which is completely written out. There is no need for me to go into any more detail than that – it would take a week! But I can assure you that, in England, both the name of the owner and the description of the property are essential to make a lease legal and enforceable. What is the property, and where is it?"

The Countess took a pamphlet from her handbag and passed it to Alex, "This is the brochure the agent gave me. As you see, it refers to a nine-room private house with four floors and a basement, in a terrace in Hampstead overlooking the Heath; the street address is given. I was captivated by it as soon as I was taken round by the agent, but I tried not to show my enthusiasm, as I thought it might give him an advantage!"

She went on, "My suspicions of the agent were first aroused when, back in his office, he said that there was no need to make any banking arrangements for payment of rent, that his clerks were able to take cash or cheques over the counter and would issue receipts accordingly. All I needed to do was to give him a letter with a statement that I had agreed to lease the property at a certain rate – 'we don't need a lease or all that mumbo-jumbo – why should the lawyers get their cut?' is what he said!"

Alex grunted, "So that they can protect the interests of both parties, that's why! A letter, such as he described, would have no legal standing whatsoever, and the landlord could have you and your effects moved out onto the street at the merest whim! I hope you have signed nothing, Countess!"

"That's the problem, Mr Crabbe – I was so taken with the place that I wrote such a letter on the agent's desk, in his office!"

"This needs following up immediately, Countess! What is the agent's name, and where are his offices?"

Chapter 29

The countess told Alex all that he needed, and he promised that he would start making enquiries the next day, "Please tell Marjorie, one of our two secretaries, where we can find you, Countess, whether or not you are staying in a hotel and whether we can reach you by telephone. She will also give you a request form to sign, which will authorise us to make enquiries on your behalf. It also lists our standard charges!"

He led her out of the back office and into the care of Marjorie for the formalities, and left her, saying, "Thank you very much for approaching us, Countess – I will telephone you as soon as I have something worthwhile to report."

After she had left, Alex turned back to Melpomene and said, "Another opportunity for you to exercise your thespian talents, Mel! This time you can be a prospective client, not an estate agent. You have seen their sign outside the house, and you are interested in taking it. I'll bet you anything you like that this dubious estate agent won't let on that he is already talking to another prospect – Countess Wybrowska!"

Melpomene decided the next morning that she would approach the estate agent exuding signs of wealth, so she selected her best tailored suit – not quite up to the standard of Stephanie Walters' Burberry, but still pretty impressive when worn over a crêpe-de-chine blouse, and accompanied by a fox fur and white silk stockings.

She parked the Alvis a few yards away from the estate agency on Hampstead Boulevard and walked to the office, which was deserted save for a thin girl completely absorbed in practicing her typewriting. By chance, a slanting beam of the sun caught the tops of the four desks, presumably used by agents, revealing to Mel's keen gaze that three of them had a layer of undisturbed dust, while only one had been recently used.

Mel rapped on the front counter and said, "Will no-one attend to me?" in a haughty voice. The typist seemed startled, jumped up and went to a glass-windowed door at the back of the office, calling, "Mr Prestwick, there's a lady!"

A thick-set man in a waistcoat and no jacket came out, wiping his walrus moustache, "Yes Madam, what can we do for you today?"

"Well, as your office proclaims itself to be a house agency, you might not be surprised to know that I wish to be shown a house!" said Mel, still in a haughty tone, but now with an edge of exasperation, "I saw your sign outside a house facing the Heath – is there any chance you would vouchsafe me a viewing – within the next hour, if at all possible?"

"Oh, certainly, certainly, Madam! Let me just get my coat and I will take you there – Julie, find me the keys, you know the ones – it's only a step, we can walk there in three minutes!"

This at least was an accurate statement, and Melpomene was soon let into the house, which indeed seemed very attractive. She made him show her every room, starting from the basement, where there was the kitchen and laundry and windows giving onto a railed off area below the front steps, and progressing, floor by floor until they reached the attic and maids' room on the top floor.

By that time, Prestwick was puffing and perspiring freely, while Melpomene took it all in her stride. Rather sadistically she made him show her each of the main reception rooms and bedrooms and offices in detail, necessitating further stair climbing, until, finally taking pity on him, she sat on a chair at the table in the formal dining room to ask him some questions.

"I noticed that the kitchen and scullery seemed not to have been used recently – how long has the house been standing vacant?"

"Less than a year, Madam, the owner has been forced to move to the country, for reasons of health, I believe. I correspond with him by letter alone, as he apparently can't abide the telephone."

"And all the furniture we have seen comes with the lease – which has a term of how many years?"

"The length of tenure can be agreed, Madam, I understand that the owner would prefer it to be at least three years, with an option for extension after that."

"A further question, Mr Prestwick, and then we should return to your office – I will need to telephone my husband before I sign the lease – I assume this will take the standard form?"

"Oh yes, Madam, we use a local solicitor to make the formal arrangements – I can take you to his office if you decide to sign up today. You said you had a further question?"

"Two questions, actually. First, am I the only person currently interested in the property? And second, I noticed a heavy padlocked door in the basement – what is that, a wine cellar?"

"Madam, you are the only prospective buyer who has shown genuine interest so far – we always have a few people making idle enquiries, of course. As for the padlocked door, I am informed that this is to a store-room where the owner keeps some items that he does not wish the tenant to use – just what, I cannot say."

Back at the estate agency, Mel asked to use the telephone privately, and was shown into Prestwick's office, while the agent left her alone. She rang Alex and said, "As we thought, there is something rotten in the state of Hampstead, but at least he has spoken about signing a lease under the supervision of a solicitor!"

"Even supposing that solicitor is genuine, too!" said Alex.

"I shall simply tell him that I need to discuss it with my husband before I can decide, Alex. But I'd really like the chance to have a look inside a mysterious locked storeroom that I saw in the basement! I'm going to try something really cheeky now, my love! Be prepared to grab some official-looking folders and I will pick you up in a few minutes!"

She went out into the main office, where Prestwick was sitting smoking a cigarette.

"My husband insists that I bring our solicitor to view the property and, if I am then convinced, to check the lease before I sign it. The lease will be in my name alone. I won't trouble you to climb those stairs any more, Mr Prestwick, so why don't I simply bring my solicitor back here, then we can take the keys and go through the house together and make notes. He is conversant with the prices of rentals that are current in this area."

Within twenty minutes, they were back at the agency. Alex was introduced as 'Mr Browning, of Browning and Steel, solicitors.' Keeping her fingers crossed, Mel asked for the keys, and was given the whole bunch, including, she noticed, a padlock key!

Chapter 30

Alex drew the Alvis up well short of the house, and turned to Melpomene before they got out of the car.

"I have the growing feeling that all this is a set-up!" he said, "The last straw for me was the way we were given all the keys, including the one for the padlock, with no question. I had suspicions before, first with the 'Countess', who seemed to be terminally naïve – not what you would expect from a woman of the world, and then when you related what had happened at the estate agent's office. What I just saw there looked to me like a hurried attempt to make a disused office look as though it was in business – that so-called typist could hardly type!"

He patted his chest, saying grimly, "So I'm glad I packed my shooter this time, baby!" and then they got out and walked up to the house.

Once inside, shutting the door behind them as quietly as possible, Alex held up his finger, indicating "hush!" and they tiptoed to the stairs leading down to the basement floor. The kitchen and scullery was dimly lit by the windows to the service area, and Alex went and unlocked the outside door.

Mel pointed to the padlocked door, and Alex unlocked it, again as quietly as possible. They looked around carefully and then pulled the door open. Beyond was darkness, but Alex felt around and found a switch near the doorway, which turned on a single bulb, hanging by its wire from the ceiling. They hung back, but could see a number of packages inside, so Alex beckoned Mel to go in. She poked around, pulled off some hessian from a large package and then came out again.

In a soft voice she said, "The one I opened was a large picture in a gilt frame – I couldn't see what the subject was. We shall have to investigate further before we have any real idea – it could be, as I was told, just the objects from the house that the owner didn't want to leave for the tenants."

Alex was just about to reply, when all the lights came on and a voice said "Caught in the act, Mr and Mrs Crabbe, what have you to say for yourselves now!" There were two men, the one who had spoken and a companion, thickset and with a walrus moustache, both wearing blue overalls and grasping long cook's knives!

Melpomene sidled away from the store-room door, past a workbench and headed towards the outside door, causing the second man to follow her, with knife held menacingly. The man who had spoken turned that way, too, and Alex grasped the edge of a heavy work table and upended it against him, making him drop his knife, which slid away under a gas cooker.

Then Alex fired a shot above the head of Mel's pursuer and shouted, "Drop the knife or I'll plug you!" The man complied with no argument or delay.

"Into the store-room with you, or, by crikey, I'll shoot you both!" shouted Alex, and both of them scuttled to safety. Mel slammed the door, and Alex snapped the padlock shut.

"Is the telephone in the hall here still connected?" asked Alex, to which Mel replied, "There is a good way of finding out!" and headed for the stairs. She picked up the telephone, had an operator answer, and asked for Jimmy Manley's number, which she knew well by now.

Someone at Mile End Road police station answered, saying that DS Manley was off duty, but could he do anything, "This is Melpomene Crabbe, you may have heard my name from Jimmy. Could you send two or three men, preferably armed, to No 5, Heathview Mansions, Hampstead, where we can present them with two desperadoes who can be detained on quite a list of charges. You could contact Jimmy at home, if that is possible, too – I'm sure he would like to be involved!"

Fifteen minutes later, a police car screeched to a halt outside the house, and a sergeant and two constables got out. Alex led them to the basement where they could hear banging from the store-room and a quavery voice saying "Let me out, I can't stand confined spaces!" to which one of the policemen said "Well, chummy, you might have to get used to them soon!"

The two were let out, handcuffed, and taken outside to await a Black Maria which had been summoned. The sergeant said, "Good work, Mr and Mrs Crabbe! You are getting quite a good reputation on the force! No hurry, you can come to the station at your own convenience to make your statements. Monday would be soon enough if you can't make it today. We can hold them on our good old charge – 'being found on enclosed premises with intent to commit a felony'. We shall see you later – I'll remember you to Jimmy – my name is George Buxton."

On the way back to the office, Alex said, "They knew our names! Now that is very interesting – I don't think I've seen either of them before – how about you, Mel?"

"No, me neither! Are we going to the office or the flat?"

"The office, because I've said I will take Marjorie and Effie to the telephone showroom – Marjorie has been making some calls to find out whether they are open and can make the arrangements for a second line, as well as showing them some of the new dial telephone models. Do you know if the local library is open on Saturdays? I want to see whether they hold a copy of the 'Almanach de Gotha' – I want to look up Countess Wybrowska, although I'm almost certain she is a fake!"

"While we're there, let's ring up David Wilkinson – we haven't spoken to him for a while and I don't want him to feel neglected!"

At the office, the two telephone seekers were ready to go, so Alex packed Effie into the Dicky seat, while Marjorie rode beside him. "See you later!" he waved, and they shot off.

Winnie was there, and Mel said, "There is no need for you to come in on Saturdays, Winnie! What are you up to?"

"Oh, I don't mind – I must confess I've been playing with new ideas for office stationery using my lovely new Royal!"

"Let me see," said Mel, "I like some of these – this one in particular, it looks dignified without being stuffy!"

"Of course, they will have different typefaces and sizes on the printed versions, I'll get the printers to make us up three or four samples to choose from. How about tinted paper?"

"Now let's not go overboard, Winnie, or we'll finish up looking like a mail-order house!"

"Of course you're right, Mel! Are you ready for a cup of tea?"

"Oh, yes indeed! And I'll tell you all about this morning and you'll know why!"

And Mel related it all to a rapt Winnie, who remarked at the end, "I always had my doubts about that so-called Countess – she was wearing an awfully cheap perfume!"

Chapter 31

When Melpomene rang David Wilkinson at Woodhampton police station, she was told "The superintendent has gone home, Madam. If it is important, do you have his home number?"

Melpomene said she had, and rang it. He answered promptly and she said, "Mel here, David. Partly social chat and partly business, if you don't mind working on a Saturday! The chit-chat can come in a moment, but the business is a matter that if you can't help me with, maybe you could tell me who to contact. I assume there is a branch of the police that deals with fraud and the like? – oh, the fraud squad, why didn't I guess! – I assume, David, that one of the things they do is keep lists of confidence tricksters. We have just had a person calling herself Countess Dorota Wybrowska trying something on with us. Does the name ring a bell?"

"Not with me, Mel, but the person you want is Chief Inspector Saunders – he runs the fraud squad; I'll tell you his direct number and the general enquiries number of the squad if he's not at his desk. Have you got something to write with?"

Mel thanked him and they turned to catching up with each other's news, trivial or more serious.

"We've been dealing with your old friend Hugo Palance again recently, David. He was able to help us thwart an attempt at inducing one of our clients to indulge in illegal activities. I'm not at liberty to say more now, but it might all come out eventually."

After twenty minutes or so of chatting, Melpomene said that she hoped to be in Woodhampton some time soon, and would certainly look him up then.

Then she tried the number of Chief Inspector Saunders, who answered the telephone himself. She introduced herself and said that David Wilkinson had given her the number, and then asked about Countess Dorota Wybrowska.

"Ah yes, she is an old customer of ours – she is really Doreen Atkinson, of the notorious Atkinson clan who run all sorts of rackets in the East End – protection and stand-over, a bit of counterfeiting, mainly of foreign banknotes that are not easily

94

recognized here, and general run-of-the-mill forgery of share certificates and so on. Oh yes, we know Doreen all right – what has she been up to now?"

Melpomene related the whole story, including the run-in with the spurious estate agent, to which Saunders replied, "You say he and his accomplice are in custody at Mile End Road – I'll give the boys there a call, maybe I can help them identify these rogues – I doubt they will have volunteered their real names."

"While we're talking, Chief Inspector, are any of these Atkinsons ever involved with art offences, such as forgery of old masters, or even auction rings and the like?"

"From time to time, yes! Just last year, the husband of Gracie, Doreen's younger sister – she's an accomplished society pickpocket – was taken in for that very activity, participating in an auction ring – his name is Liversedge."

"Well, well!" said Mel, "You may be interested to know that he was at it again only a few days ago – I myself was instrumental in getting him and some associates locked up over an auction ring in Berkshire!"

"Can you tell me the names of the others?" asked Saunders.

Mel thought for a moment, and then decided she was not passing on sensitive information, since it was no secret that they had been charged, "Apart from Andrew Liversedge, there was Henry Arthur Winton, Martin Wilmot and Keith Satterfield – do any of these sound familiar to you?"

"I would have to look up our files, Mrs Crabbe, they don't ring any immediate bells. Give me a number where you can be reached, and I'll get back to you."

Mel thanked him effusively and told him the flat and office numbers.

She only had time for one cup of Lapsang Souchong and a jam tart when the others arrived back, Effie proudly carrying two cardboard boxes by the strings round them. "We can't use these yet until they put in the lines, but here we've got the very latest telephones! I'll take one out, the box has already been opened at the shop!"

She demonstrated the instrument, much like the ordinary telephone, with an earpiece on a cord and the mouthpiece on the top of a 'candle-stick' standard, but with a dial at its base.

"I can't wait to use it!" she said, "But they can't come and do the wiring until Monday or Tuesday."

"And you will be going home tomorrow, as soon as your father comes," Marjorie reminded her.

Effie's face dropped a little, but she said, "I hope I can come here again, lots!"

"As long as you don't miss any more school!" said Alex, "If you complete your education, and perhaps go to University, we may have a vacancy for you here! But of course you can come here in the holidays, if your father can spare you, and as long as you promise to help us out!"

Said Mel, "Don't forget we are all going to the pictures tonight! The performance starts at eight, what shall we do about eating?"

After discussion, it was decided that their favourite Italian restaurant would be the best choice.

"Oh good!" said Effie, "Will they have spaghetti?"

And, as she found out, they did!

The meal and chat were all very pleasant, and when the time came to call a taxi for the cinema they were all feeling a little somnolent, so that Effie exclaimed, "I hope the picture is very exciting, it would be a waste to go there and fall asleep!"

It turned out that she needn't have worried, she was entranced by the dog-fight scenes, Alex fell in love with Clara Bow all over again despite her widely-criticized Brooklyn accent, and the girls were divided over the male leads, Winifred and Marjorie preferring Richard Arlen, and Melpomene and Effie going for Buddy Rogers.

"No wonder they awarded it one of those new Oscars!" said Melpomene as they left the theatre, "and, as I said after seeing 'The Jazz Singer', I predict that there will be no silent films at all after the next two or three years!"

When they got back to the flat, there was a note from Caroline saying that Arthur Ralston had called and expected to be back at Tilbury at about mid-day, and would telephone as soon as he had arrived home.

After cups of chocolate, and some more talk, they all went to bed and dreamed of being in the movies.

Chapter 32

Everybody slept in a bit after arriving back home past midnight – they had needed to wait quite a while for a taxi – but one by one they straggled out to a comprehensive breakfast. Since they felt they should stay at home until Arthur Ralston rang, they spent their time in various ways. Mel, of course, did the Sunday Times crossword, which was always a particularly difficult one, and Alex and Effie played pencil-and-paper games, such as boxes and noughts-and-crosses. Effie invariably won, but when challenged on this, Alex denied that he had been letting her win, "That would be as bad as cheating!" he exclaimed.

Finally, at 11.30, Arthur Ralston rang, saying that he had just disembarked but thought he might go and talk to the customs people, some of whom he knew quite well through dealing with them over the years, "I'll possibly spend an hour with them and then I'll pick up my car from where I parked it next to the wharf and drive home – let me see, that means I shall be getting home about 1 o'clock. Can I have a word with Effie, please?"

Effie was very happy after talking to her father, "He says he has a present for me, but I told him that seeing him again would be enough of a present! But I still wonder what he's brought me!"

"If you like, Effie, Melpomene or I will drive you home so you will be there when he arrives, how about that?"

"Oh, yes please! Can I travel in front this time? I like the Dicky seat, but that will make a nice change!"

"Right you are, Mel will take you, at about 12.30. OK?"

When they got to the house, Effie said, "The car's not here yet, but we've got the house keys, so we can go in and put the kettle on. I don't suppose Daddy will be very long."

She was right, the kettle was still boiling when Arthur came in and gave Effie a hug. He handed her a small package, and she kissed him and unwrapped it, to find a snow-globe with the Eiffel Tower inside. She shook it to make a snowstorm and then kissed him again.

"Now, Melpomene, I have something for you too, but nothing as tangible as a snow-globe," said Arthur, "I had an exceedingly interesting conversation with the Senior Preventive Officer in the Customs Office at Tilbury. I told him, in general terms, about the threatening proposition made to me, and explained that so far only the minor elements of the gang had been arrested, but that investigations were still in progress on the French side. I did not, of course, want to interfere with any detective activities, official or otherwise, but I gave him the name and number of your agency and said that I thought you would be glad to cooperate with his service – I hope I did right!"

"You certainly did!" said Mel, "Perhaps you could give me his name and telephone number, too. It's quite possible that smuggling is an important part of the illicit art trade. The more that various investigative bodies work together, the more likely they are to be successful."

"Now," said Melpomene, "we found last time we were here that there were hardly any groceries in the house, and we had to resort to fish and chips – which I, for one, rather enjoyed! I don't suppose there are many shops open on a Sunday round here, are there?"

"Probably not," said Arthur, "but Effie and I sometimes go and eat at a nice little Indian place in the High Street, so you have no need to worry that we will go hungry! Thank you very much for looking after my little girl – I'm immensely grateful!"

"It was a great pleasure, I assure you – she is welcome at any time! Bear that in mind if you have occasion to be away from home in the future! Now, I'd better go home and leave you two to share your tales of adventure!"

She kissed and hugged Effie, whose eyes were sparkling with tears, and found that she too, had to dab at her eyes a little as she got into the Alvis.

When she returned to the office, she was greeted by Alex, who said, "Some people are very eager! I have just been talking to Ben Fisher, the Senior Preventive Officer of Customs at Tilbury, who telephoned because he is very keen to share information with us. He is particularly interested, of course, in anything we can glean from questioning our Mr Considine. I told him that I would ring Jimmy Manley at Mile End Road in the morning, to discover whether they have been able to get anything out of him yet, and that I would give Jimmy his name and number. Ben tells me that they have had cases before of illicit goods being added to legitimate consignments, even while they were in bond. The inference he made was that there were one or two dubious officers in HM Customs, even though they have exhaustive procedures to eliminate them. He can recall that his immediate predecessor in the job had a bonded warehouseman dismissed and charged ten years or so ago, for undoing seals and introducing bottles of liqueur into packing cases of furniture destined for Germany. He promised he would go through his records for anything of an art nature."

"That was very quick!" said Mel, "It must have been only a couple of hours ago, at most, that Arthur was telling him about his experiences! First, Alex, I need a cup of tea! – And then we must talk about our program for tomorrow. I'll ring Stephanie Walters in the morning, and if she is agreeable, I thought I could take Winnie and her pet Royal to Northampton – we'll have to stop off at her flat so that she can pack some clothing for her stay. And you will probably want to hang around in case the telephone people want to do their installation."

"Oh, you're right," said Alex, "but if anything turns up for me, calling me out of the office, I'd be happy for Marjorie to deal with the telephone business. If we do get a second line tomorrow, I'll call one or two key people – Hugo especially, and Jimmy, too – and let them know the number."

As promised, Mel rang Stephanie at her police station in the morning, "Hello, Stephanie, how was your tennis on Saturday? Ah well, two sets to love is pretty good! I was thinking of bringing Winnie up later this morning, we have to pick up some of her things. Would that be all right? I'll bring her straight to your house – now, now, Stephanie, leaving a key under the mat is hardly what I'd expect from a professional like you! See you later!"

As soon as Winnie arrived at the office, Melpomene put her straight into the Alvis and drove to her flat. One of her two flatmates was there, and Mel was introduced to her, "Melpomene Crabbe, please meet Maureen Castle – she is the photographer I told you about."

Maureen was a rather hefty young woman – Mel wondered whether she might be a hockey player – but she had a shy smile and a quiet demeanour.

Winnie grabbed a bag for her things – the typewriter was already in the Dicky seat – and they were soon heading North.

Chapter 33

On the drive, Mel and Winnie chatted about various topics – what Winnie could do with information that Stephanie might have gathered and not sorted through yet. "You know, Winnie, this is similar to what any efficient secretary already does with correspondence, for instance – thinking up useful categories and headings, and then deciding where to file the individual letters."

"And, I suppose," responded Winnie, "you might want to put additional copies in different files, so that a letter might be filed with Mr Smith's stuff and also in pending orders."

"Exactly!" said Mel, "The main thing is to keep an open mind and look for relationships. This is what social anthropology is all about, too!"

They talked about other things, too, Mel asked, "Your friend Maureen looks as though she could be a hockey player – something athletic anyway?"

"You're nearly right, Mel! She plays lacrosse in the Regent Street Poly Firsts – they even play men's teams sometimes, because there are not too many lacrosse clubs around the London area."

The miles passed quickly with all this talking, and soon they pulled up outside Stephanie's house. Mel ran up the front path and, looking round to make sure she was not observed, lifted up the doormat. There was no key there, but an envelope addressed to 'Miss Morris', which she took back to the car and gave to Winnie. Inside was a note:

'Dear Winnie, I thought I would start our collaboration with a test of your deductive powers! Please do not take offence, this is meant to be friendly! My riddle for you is this: My first is in 'sugar' but not in 'budgerigar'. My next is in 'heaven' but not in 'adventure'. My third is in 'meat' but not in 'mulatto' and my last is in 'dove' but not in 'overcoat'. See if you can find what you are looking for, now!'

Winnie pondered for no more than half a minute, then gave a laugh and disappeared through the side gate into the back garden. Melpomene waited, read through the note and nodded with a grin. Then Winnie came back through the gate beaming, and brandishing a key, as Melpomene said, "It was in the shed, wasn't it?" They both laughed happily.

Mel showed Winnie the room she would occupy, and they set up the typewriter on the desk. There was already a couple of reams of paper, a packet of carbon paper and some pens, as well as a box of file cards.

Winnie said. "Excellent! But she has forgotten scissors, a typing eraser, an ordinary rubber eraser, and a ruler!" Then she pulled open the drawer and said, "My apologies, she hasn't forgotten after all, there's even a pencil sharpener! Looks like we two will get on very well!"

Melpomene said, "I can vouch for the comfort of the sofa-bed – can you see how it unfolds?"

Just then they heard the front door being opened, and Stephanie knocked at Winnie's door, saying, "Can I come in, Winnie?" The two were introduced, with kisses, and each looked very pleased with their future colleague.

"This calls for cups of tea," said Stephanie, "and I bought an apple tea-cake on my way here!"

Over tea, the conversation soon turned to substantive matters. Winnie was handed a box file, which Stephanie explained held as much information as she had been able to accumulate on the dubious guests at the Hendersons' dinner party, and a second one covering names that had come up since.

"I was able to put real names to most of those who were caught by you at the auction ring, Melpomene. As you know, some of them, particularly Keith Satterfield, are old customers, but those with no prior convictions were harder to place. I'm still working on it, though. When Niels Mortensen gets here from Copenhagen, I hope he will bring us more names and more information. By the way, have you or Alex had a chance to visit the Wimbledon house where Satterfield is thought to reside – or at least, where he keeps his car?"

"Not yet, Stephanie," said Melpomene, "but it's on our list! While I think of it, we've made two new contacts who may be useful, Chief Inspector Saunders, of the Fraud Squad and a Customs official, Senior Preventive Officer Ben Fisher, based at Tilbury Docks. Winnie has their numbers, I think. CI Saunders told us about the Atkinson clan – an extensive family of assorted criminals, ranging from one who he calls a 'society pickpocket' – who I suppose is a well-dressed lady who circulates at balls, opera performances and the races – to confidence tricksters like the Countess Wybrowska – real name Doreen Atkinson – who Alex and I recently encountered as part of an attempt at real-estate fraud. A member by marriage of that clan we have already run into, Andrew Liversedge, one of the dinner-party cabal who we also nabbed over the auction ring. Talk about 'wheels within wheels'!"

"Yes, I have him under the microscope, as well as the Satterfields, but we still haven't got any leads on the big boys in this field," added Stephanie, "I would be surprised if there were not one or two fat spiders sitting in the middle of a web somewhere!"

"Like Pilkington!" exclaimed Mel, "Perhaps you read about him – he was one of Crabbe and Crabbe's biggest catches, so far. That reminds me – I don't know whether we have just been lucky so far, but we haven't run into any real violence yet in the criminal art world. Perhaps these crims are more refined!"

"Cross your fingers when you say such things!" said Stephanie, "What I have found in my work over the years is that once someone has put their feet on the slippery path, they throw off all pretensions to being decent and civilized – a crook is a crook is a crook!"

"You're right," said Mel, "we had knives brandished at us the other day at the house we were lured to by Countess Wyborska – that could have led to real violence, had Alex not scared them off with a warning shot from his Luger – which reminds me about yet another lead we haven't followed up yet – there was a locked strong-room in that house. I was able to have a peep at one item in there, and it was a large picture in a gilded frame! We need to go back there, sooner rather than later!"

"I don't know about you two," said Stephanie, "but all this talk has given me an appetite! I can make some omelettes, or I can treat you to the delights of the Northampton police canteen, which is it to be?"

"Omelettes!" said Mel and Winnie, almost in unison! And, as they said later, it was the right choice! "Are we going to take turns cooking?" Winnie asked Stephanie, "I don't get many chances at my flat, we haven't got much of a kitchen there, just a gas-ring and a toaster!"

Chapter 34

Mel asked whether she could use the telephone to check whether there had been anything interesting at the office, however the operator said, "I'm sorry, Madam, that line appears to be out of service. Please try again later."

"Oh, I know!" she said, "I bet the telephone installers are on the job! Never mind, I'll just go back and see how things are. You might try to ring in an hour, Winnie, and if you get through, just tell them I'm on my way. I'll talk to you both later – don't work too hard, but make what you do count!"

When she arrived back, the telephone people were clearing up, and there were two shining new dial telephones! The installer said, "You still have the same number as before – it would cause chaos if we had to change it! But here on this card is your extra number – I would advise you to tell it to everyone you call frequently – but you can decide who yourselves."

The first incoming call – on the old number of course – was from Anatole, who said, "Alex, can I come round right away – I have some news that I think will interest you a lot!"

He arrived twenty minutes later, in a state of some excitement, so Marjorie made him sit down with a cup of tea and a jam tart. He was so eager to start that he swallowed some crumbs the wrong way and had to have his back thumped.

"It all started first thing this morning. Severin asked me to arrange for the two large seascapes he bought the other day at Sedgwick Manor – you may vaguely remember that day! – to be picked up and brought to the gallery, as they were too big for the Rolls. So I phoned Pickfords, who said that they could do it, but that I would have to go to their office and give them the details and then accept their quote for the job. And they said that if the goods were valuable they needed to be insured or accompanied by the consignee or a representative – in other words, me!"

"And of course, this was the case," said Alex, "as I recall there was a sum of over a thousand guineas involved!"

"That's right! So I went to their depot with an authorization letter from Severin, and started to give them the details. I asked the man at the counter whether they knew where Sedgwick

103

Hall was, and he burst out laughing, saying that it took them three days to get their van back from there last time, because the police had impounded it and were scouring it for fingerprints of some crooks who had been mixed up in a fraud!"

"I asked whether they had checked up on the people who'd booked it, but he said that all four of them had given names and addresses that turned out to be false, so there was no point. 'We're hauliers, not detectives!' he said."

"Anyway," went on Anatole, "I turned up at the depot that afternoon to go to the Hall, as arranged, and on the way down the driver was quite chatty, so I asked him if he'd been the one who had his van impounded and he said he was, and when he had asked the police how he was going to get home they said that was not their concern, it was up to him! So he was a bit sour with them and didn't let on where he'd picked the four crooks up to take them down to Sedgwick Hall that morning. I asked him whether he would tell me, and he said, sure, he had no quarrel with me! So he wrote the address down. We picked up the seascapes and took them to the gallery, then he ran me back to the depot to pick up my Morris 8, and I slipped him the price of a few beers!"

"Did you have a look at the place?" asked Melpomene, but Anatole shook his head, "I thought I had better not muddy the waters for you, as I knew you had been trying very hard to locate some of these people! Anyway, here is the address – Pengelly House, Fairford Avenue, Wimbledon."

Alex whistled, "This is a very familiar address to us, Anatole! Mel and I shall certainly have to pay it a visit – armed to the teeth, I would think! These gentlemen seem to have a liking for big knives!"

"Thanks a lot, Anatole!" said Mel, "We might make a detective of you yet, to add to all your other skills!"

She walked him to the door and kissed him on the cheek, causing him to blush!

"Now, Alex, let me take you up on this 'armed to the teeth' thing. I've been pondering this, and I think I will take up your suggestion of getting a Beretta or similar small gun that will go in a handbag. I don't think ladies are the right shape for shoulder holsters! I believe that David Wilkinson paved the way for you at the Firearms Registry at Scotland Yard, did he not? I will get onto him shortly and see if he can do the same for me."

"Meanwhile, Mel, one or both of us might take an alternative approach and visit the house in an assumed character – if the forces of evil can do it, so can we, can't we?"

"As long as I can have a change of profession, Alex, I'm somewhat bored with being an estate agent! Let me see – what if we try door-to-door selling? No – come to think of it, that might ruin our chances from the very beginning!"

"Evangelists? No. Insurance salesmen? No – worse than door-to-door encyclopedias! Private detectives? No – who needs 'em? I've got it, Alex, pest exterminators – but we'd need to have convincing-looking equipment, or little dogs at least! Think!, Alex, think!"

"I need another cup of tea first! I'll think afterwards!"

Marjorie had been listening, and went to put the kettle on. When she had done this, she said, "You know, we had a visitor here a couple of weeks ago – we accepted his explanation immediately and welcomed him in without question – and he had an assistant with him – don't you remember? That would be an ideal role, you wouldn't be suspected for a minute!"

"Oh, come on, Marjorie!" said Melpomene, "Put us out of our misery, do! – I've got no idea who you are talking about!"

"You'll kick yourself when I tell you – which goes to show what a good idea this is! What he said was, roughly, 'Good morning Madam, North London Gas Company – come to read your meter, and we're checking all households for leaky appliances.' – Now do you remember?"

"Wonderful!" said Mel, "Alex can wear blue overalls and I can have something like a police-woman's uniform, with a badge saying 'Gas' and a thick notebook and be the one in charge! And we'll need some sort of a gadget with a nozzle and a little meter on it, for detecting the leaks!"

"And I know just where we can get such a gadget!" said Alex, "From the local garage – we can borrow or buy the sort of tyre gauge they use for lorries – all we have to do is replace the bit that goes onto the tyre valve with some little funnel thing!"

"So that's what we'll buy next – overalls, tunic and a gadget!"

Chapter 35

The next morning as soon as they were back in the office, Melpomene and Alex started thinking where they should go to buy what they needed for the expedition to the Wimbledon house.

"This is only a single occasion, for the moment, anyway," said Alex, "so it would seem a bit extravagant to buy new stuff – why don't we try the second-hand places?"

"Of course!" said Mel, "This is often great fun as well. How about the Portobello Road – there is a huge range of different places there, ranging from a stall I must admit I used to patronize as a student, where you can get high-fashion dresses that rich women refuse to wear more than once, to second-hand bookshops and ones selling bric-a-brac of all kinds. Let's go now!"

"But we'll need to watch ourselves, Mel, otherwise we'll come home with armfuls of stuff we don't really need! We should get the items we really need first, and only then start looking around for bargains!"

After only a short ride, Mel parked the Alvis in a side-street off the main thoroughfare and they started wandering past the houses and shops to where there were groups of stalls and barrows, with sellers and costermongers shouting the merits of their wares. Mel stopped first at a stall with service uniforms, but her rummaging was unsuccessful. However, the third or fourth stall of that kind had navy-blue jackets with metal buttons that she thought would pass for a gas inspector's uniform. She soon found one that fitted, and twirled for Alex's approval. He gave her the thumbs up, so she bought it.

"Now I need a narrow skirt to match, maybe a cap, and some sensible shoes, which I haven't had since I was at school!" she said, and they kept their eyes open for these while Alex looked for a set of blue overalls, which didn't take him long.

Within an hour they had everything on their list, except for the 'gadget', so they took a break to have a snack from the wide selection on offer from stalls. Mel had jellied eels, while Alex chose a meat pie with peas. Both meals were washed down with strong sweet tea from enamel mugs.

They had worked their way along almost the full length of Portobello Road, so they crossed over and started walking back. On this side there were mainly shops, rather than stalls, and Alex soon found a shop selling all kinds of electrical and plumbing supplies. He picked through the goods and bought what looked like suitable components for constructing the 'gadget'.

"Now we can buy for pleasure, not business!" Melpomene announced, and darted immediately into a shop with its window full of everything from miniature plaster replicas of the Venus de Milo to clocks and a few small pictures. Inside there were more pictures, in varying stages of decay, but then she spotted something which made her nudge Alex and whisper in his ear.

She picked up a framed etching, about ten inches by eight, and examined it closely. It had a paper sticker saying £3/10/0 on the back, so she went to the proprietor, a rather corpulent woman and asked, "Have you got any more of these old things, love? I've got a place along by my stairs that I need to fill up. I'll give you a good price if you've got more all the same size."

The woman looked at it and said, "I do believe I 'ave, dear – now where did I put 'em?" She rummaged through some cardboard boxes and came up with six more. "That's about it, dear! How about twenty-five pounds for the lot?"

"Make it twenty-two and you've got a deal!" said Mel, "Can you throw in a box for them?"

"Certainly, dear, and I'll even tie it up with string – no extra charge!" and she laughed cheerily.

While she was doing that, Mel asked, in an offhand way, "How do you pick up all this stuff?"

"Oh," was the reply, "some of it I picks up at estate sales, some gets brought in by people down on their luck, and some comes from men who don't want no questions asked! I couldn't tell you how I got this lot, it was a year or more ago."

Mel paid, thanked the woman, and she and Alex headed back to the Alvis. Mel lingered at one or two more shops, but Alex dissuaded her from any more 'bargains'.

As soon as they were back at the office, Melpomene rang Stephanie Walters at Northampton police station, saying,

"Remember you told me about those etchings that Satterfield and Barker were suspected of stealing? You said that the details were circulated with no result. Could you look up those details for me? I have just bought some etchings in the Portobello Road for much less that they must be worth. Let me describe one for you and then you can see whether it might be one of the missing batch. It is about ten by eight, like those that were pinched. It is a scene of what looks like a ruined abbey, the title is 'Priorat in Schottland' and the artist's name is Chodowiecki, which sounds more Polish than German, but what would I know! There is a number 6/8 written by hand after the title, which I suppose means that it is the sixth print of a total of eight. Is that enough for you to look it up, Stephanie?"

"More than enough, I should say, Mel! I'll look it up right away and ring you back."

"We have two numbers, now, Stephanie! And I just dialled yours, instead of having to go through the operator! Can you write our second number down?"

While she was doing this, Alex was fiddling about with the 'gadget' using the parts he had bought and a lavish amount of black electrical tape. He showed it to Marjorie, who agreed it would convince anyone but a gas fitter. He applied it to the tap at the side of the gas ring and tried to look wise as he read the dial.

"Now for my uniform!" said Mel, putting on a slim navy-blue skirt, thick black lisle stocking and lace-up flat shoes, the jacket, which buttoned up to the neck, with no need for a shirt collar or tie, and finally a cap like the ones that the clippies were wearing on the buses.

"That looks pretty business-like," said Alex, "it would be good if you had a badge, too, but I suppose we can't have everything! If we're going to Wimbledon tomorrow, we'd better work out some sort of basic plan this evening at home, around which we can improvise as the situation demands. I'm only the technician, so you will have to do most of the talking, of course – I don't suppose that will worry you, dear!"

"I shall ignore that crack, Alex! I think I'll wear this outfit back to the flat, and see what effect is has on Caroline and Mrs M! I need to get accustomed to it in any case, so that I appear to move naturally – I especially need to get used to these clumpy shoes!"

Chapter 36

Mel had some ideas about the Wimbledon visit, "First, Alex, we had better check what gas company they have there – it would be a bit of a give-away if we said we were from North London Gas and they really get theirs from another company! Then, I've had another thought – we could go next door first, with the same story, so we can rehearse our act and also to see if they will tell us anything about the neighbours. If we're feeling up to it, we could do this at the next-door houses both sides. You never know, we could pick up something useful."

"Yes!" said Alex, "And the doors will probably be opened by maids or someone – it seems a fairly affluent area – and servants are often a good source of gossip! Let's do it!"

They drove to the flat, and Melpomene got a gratifying reaction from Caroline, "You haven't joined the Fire Service, have you? But you will have to do something about your blonde curls, Mel, they are peeping out all around your cap and destroying the effect!"

"I'll grease them down with some of Alex' brilliantine – that will make my hair seem darker, too. And Alex is not going to shave, so he'll look a bit scruffy! But the clothes are what will put people off the scent who might have only seen us once or twice, with any luck – we shall see! It's a pity I haven't got a Gas Company badge to wear, but I don't suppose people pay too much attention to that."

Straight after breakfast they drove to Fairford Avenue, passed Pengelly House and parked some way down the road. Then they walked back toward their destination and found that the house next door was called Tavistock Lodge. It was not so grand as Pengelly House, but still substantial and well-kept, with a gravel drive to the front door.

Fortunately, Mel noticed a sign directing them to the Tradesmen's Entrance before they rang at the front door, so they went round the side of the house, found it and knocked.

A thin woman in an apron opened it, saying "What is it?" and Mel went into her spiel, remembering that they were from East Surrey Gas, to which the woman responded, "So where's Ernie Potts got to, then?"

Mel thought fast, "The company is trying out women inspectors, as you see, so you'll have to show us where everything is. Mr Potts has been shifted to Head Office for now."

"All right, you'd better come in, then. The meter is under the stairs, I'll take you – you said you're checking for leaks, too, so I'll show you the kitchen and the laundry, we've got a gas copper down there. There used to be gas lights here, but when the electric came through they took 'em all out – but maybe the pipes is still here."

Mel pretended to read the meter, and wrote some figures down in her thick black book, and Alex tested every appliance and gas-tap he was shown, and Mel noted his results too. He said, "I can see they've disconnected the line for the lights at the meter, Missus, so no need to go through the house checking them. Are there any gas fires in the bedrooms and such?"

"No, we've got those electric ones now – can't say as I feel as warm with them as with a real fire with flames!"

They thanked the woman and said there would be a letter from Head Office with the next bill. They left and headed for Pengelly House.

"Are we going to have another practice run?" asked Alex, "No," said Mel, "I reckon we picked up enough just now – I'm jolly glad we did it, though! Let's see if Pengelly House has a tradesmen's entrance, too!"

It did, so they rang the bell there and were greeted by an elderly man with whiskers, wearing a green baize apron.

"What can I do for you, Miss?" he said, "I'm just in the middle of doing the boots and shoes."

"We're from East Surrey Gas, Ernie Potts has been transferred to Head Office, and the company is trying out women inspectors – they don't have to pay us as much as the men – so I'll read the meters, and Albert here will check all your appliances for leaks. Are there any residents in the house now – we don't want to cause any disturbance – and there might be gas fires and such in rooms that they are occupying?"

"I'd better ask the butler, Arthur, to check if it's all right. There's a big meeting going on in the dining-room and there's a gas ban-mary and a plate-warmer on the sideboard in there, as well as a gas fire. I'll show you where the meter is, and then I'll get Arthur to inform you whether you can go in and do your checking."

As he left them by the meter cupboard and disappeared up the stairs, Mel said quietly, "We might have been given a bonus here, Alex! Keep your head down in case there are any old acquaintances about!"

The butler, a tall dignified personage, came down the stairs and toward them, wringing his hands somewhat anxiously. "I have asked Sir and Madam, and they say you can come in to the dining-room, as long as you are very quick and don't cause any commotion – they are holding a business meeting. Please follow me!"

He knocked softly on a door, ushered Mel and Alex in and took them to the long sideboard where there was a bain-marie and a plate warmer, both turned on. There was a pile of used plates there, and several scattered about the table, evidently the remains of a late working breakfast.

At the head of the table was a bald man, who they both recognised immediately as Keith Satterfield, alias Burton, and sitting next to him was the mysterious Eliza Stanford! Fortunately neither of them were looking at the gas inspectors. Satterfield was giving the butler more instructions, and Eliza was intently reading some documents in front of her. Mel and Alex made sure not to look too obviously at the people round the table, but while Alex did his testing, they each took surreptitious peeps, while Mel wrote notes in her black book.

Alex tried to spin out his testing as long as he could, but after a while, the butler came over to them and said, "Will you be finished soon? The Master and Mistress want to get on with their meeting, which is highly confidential."

Mel said, "We are nearly done, please apologise for us. The work has to be done – I'm sure that nobody wants the gas to be cut off for major work!"

As they went to leave the room, which needed them to skirt the full length of one side of the table, they tried to see if they could make out what was on any of the documents. At the door, they paused and asked the butler to give their apologies once again, and then left the room.

Back in the Alvis, they both burst out laughing, mainly in relief!

Chapter 37

After a mile or so, Alex pulled over, saying, "We'd better try and make detailed notes of what we just saw, otherwise we might forget some of it. Have you got your big book ready?"

"Well," said Mel, "it was a good idea to go into next door first, as it sorted out our performances for the real event – but we didn't get anything from the housekeeper, or whoever she was. I had hoped to pick up some gossip there. Never mind, we certainly got some good information from Pengelly House itself, and we can always go back and do the house on the other side later."

"So," replied Alex, "we have confirmed that Keith Satterfield and the enigmatic Eliza Stanford both live there. And I think I saw at least two of the other auction ring people, Andrew Liversedge – who was called Smith on the day, and Martin Wilmot, or Brown."

"Yes, as soon as I spotted them I averted my gaze!" said Mel, "Since it was me that caught them they might have remembered me, although I did slam the van door on them pretty promptly! So, all in all, we have confirmed that Pengelly House is the headquarters of the auction ring branch of the gang, and we have also proved a link between them and the Atkinson clan in Limehouse, and therefore with Countess Wybrowska and her side-kicks. I wonder if the police have got anything from those two? And we should go and have a look at that strong-room before long, before they let that house to a genuine tenant! Oh, crikey, we were supposed to go to the station and give evidence about those two, weren't we! We had better ring Sergeant Buxton as soon as we get home."

"Did you manage to see anything on the papers they were looking at just now, Mel? I tried but without success – I could hardly stop and peer over their shoulders!"

"Me neither, Alex! But I can feel lunch coming on, I wonder if any workman's caff around here serves gas inspectors? Stop if you see somewhere likely!"

They found a place that served sausages and mash, and soon quelled their hunger pangs.

When they arrived back at the flat, Caroline said, "You'd better telephone Marjorie before she gets cross with you – she says she's had a stream of messages – let me see – Jimmy Manley, Winnie in Northampton, your Mama, Mel, and Stephen Buckmaster in Woodhampton so far this morning!"

"OK, Alex – can you deal with this?" said Mel, "If I don't have a bath and wash this gunk out of my hair straight away I shall go completely bonkers!"

Alex rang Marjorie and assured her he would follow up those calls, "Meanwhile," she said, "I've had a bizarre message from a reporter on the 'Surrey Examiner' – apparently a local paper that covers Wimbledon and surrounding places. He wanted your comment on a story he intends to run tomorrow. He read it to me and I took it down – you might be intrigued, shall I read it to you, or do you want to do the telephoning first?"

"Save it for us, please, Marjorie, Mel's in the bath anyway!"

Alex rang Jimmy first, finding that he was killing two birds with one stone, because Jimmy wanted to know when they would come and give evidence about the knife-wielding goons, "By the way, since they were both regular customers, we were able to identify them through fingerprint records, even though they gave false names at first. One is called Terence Forbes, and the one with the moustache who was pretending to be an estate agent is an Atkinson – Francis of that ilk. So, with your help, we'll be able to charge them with a number of offences – common assault, assault with a deadly weapon, use of threats to obtain advantage, attempted fraud – and even practicing as an estate agent without a licence!"

Mel emerged from the bathroom at that point, with her hair wrapped in a towel, and called her Mama, who was simply making one of her regular checks to see that they were all well and uninjured, Mel reassured her and promised to visit Woodhampton in the not-too-distant future.

Alex told her about the message from the reporter, and Mel said that she would like to hear what it was all about, so rang Marjorie.

"Right!" she said, "I'll read it to you – I got it all down I think. Here goes: 'WARNING TO HOUSEHOLDERS. Peter Potter, police roundsman. Householders in the Wimbledon area and adjacent suburbs should be alert for bogus gas inspectors who are working in

113

the area, possibly casing residences for later burglary attempts. A genuine inspector from the East Surrey Gas Company, Mr Ernest Potts, called at a residence in Fairford Avenue, Wimbledon on his normal rounds, only to be told that the house had already been visited by a woman, who had said that the company was now employing female inspectors and that Mr Potts had been transferred to Head Office. Our informant, Mr Arthur Rowlands, the butler, told this reporter that he had suspected the woman and her accomplice, a shifty-looking man in dirty overalls, from the beginning, and said that they were unduly curious for gas workers and had poked into things that shouldn't have concerned them.'

He told me that there was a related article that would be run in a box next to the first item: *'SCHOOLGIRL'S ALERT SIGHTING. Peter Potter, police roundsman. A student from a prestigious local girls' academy, Miss Angelica Frazer-Smith, telephoned this paper to report what she thought might be a significant sighting. She had been walking home along Wimbledon High Street, having become indisposed at school, when she saw an interesting car parked outside a café. She is very interested in motors and told this reporter that her father, Sir Reginald Frazer-Smith, owns a brand-new Bentley, while her mother drives a high-performance Italian two-seater, an Isotta-Fraschini, which she often races on the Continent. So when Miss Frazer-Smith saw an Alvis 14 duck-tailed roadster parked there, she wanted to have a good look at it. While she was doing that, two persons came out of the café and got into the car. 'I didn't think they looked like the sort of people to own an Alvis, the woman was very untidy-looking, with a jacket that didn't fit properly and a skirt that didn't match, and the man was a low-class working person in a boiler-suit. So I took down the number, which I have just told the police, in case they had stolen the car.' Since the young lady's description corresponded with that of the spurious gas inspectors, this reporter contacted an acquaintance at the local station, who promised to follow up the number and make sure that the real owners were informed.'*

"What do you think of that!" said Marjorie, "Rather amusing, don't you think, Mel!"

"It may be amusing, but it is also alarming!" said Melpomene, "I bet the villains at Pengelly House read the local paper, and now the Alvis will be a marked car throughout the criminal fraternity! As we have sometimes thought in the past, Marjorie, our dear little Alvis is becoming a liability to Crabbe and Crabbe, and we may have to consider very seriously whether or not to replace it – however distressing that will be!"

Chapter 38

Melpomene carried on with the list of telephone calls. Next, she rang Winnie, in Northampton, who told her she was getting on very well with Stephanie and that they had combined their lists of suspects. "We are getting the real names of quite a few," she said, "mainly from finger-print records, and in some cases we have found connections between them that were not apparent before, so that will be valuable. On that point, we are still puzzled about the other dinner guests, Perkins and Benson – their connections haven't emerged yet, if there are any. Of course they might be independent operators, but it seems unlikely. By the way, Niels Mortensen has been in touch with Stephanie, and he is coming here in a couple of days. He won't be staying in the house, Steph has found him a nice guest-house only a few doors away. That's about all I have to report, Mel, is there anything else you want to tell us?"

"Yes, Winnie, a bit more about the puzzling Satterfields. We found through the car registration that William's address is Pengelly House, but when we were there this morning, the one we saw was Keith, who we remembered from the auction ring! I'll tell you and Stephanie everything about our visit another time, except that the ones there today included Keith Satterfield, Eliza Stanford, Andrew Liversedge, aka Smith, and Martin Wilmot, or Brown, as well as several others. Perhaps this might add to your lists of connections. By the way, when I'm up your way next time, I'll talk to you about sociograms, which have proved very useful in social anthropology and might be valuable for us. We must keep in touch, Winnie!"

The last one on Marjorie's list to be rung was Stephen Buckmaster. He was not there when Mel called, but his secretary said she would ask him to ring back as soon as he came out of court, "Mainly traffic offences today – nothing very exciting happens here when you are out of town, Mrs Crabbe!"

Mel took the opportunity to leave her second office number, thanked her and rang off, when immediately it rang again – it was Stephanie Walters this time.

"Winnie tells me she just brought you up to date to some extent, Mel," she said, "but she didn't know the outcome of my search of the lists of missing or stolen artworks. I checked for etchings with the title or artist of the one you told me about, and – lo and behold – I found it listed among the ones that Satterfield and Barker were briefly accused of stealing, eleven in all – you will recall that neither the pictures or any conclusive evidence were found at the time. Rather than me trying to describe them all over the telephone, why don't you bring yours up here when you come the next time, and we can do a proper job of checking them off? It's a pity that the dealer you bought yours from had no recollection of who sold them to her, so the trail is lost. That's the trouble with second-hand shops – registered art dealers are supposed to keep full records – not that they always do, of course!"

As she was thanking Stephanie and ringing off, Melpomene put her finger on a couple of unspoken questions that had been in the back of her mind for a while – how had the villains at the Hampstead house known their names? – and how had the reporter on the 'Surrey Examiner' known which number to telephone when he read Marjorie his stories?

"Its the Alvis again!" she exclaimed to Alex, "That reporter found out our address from the police, who had been given the car's registration number by the alert Miss Frazer-Smith! Once he had that, the telephone number was easy. But that doesn't explain how the Hampstead pair knew who we were – this is a bit of a puzzle!"

"The same way!" said Alex, "You parked the car outside the pretend estate agency and spent a while telephoning me and so on. He could have popped out, or sent his girl out, to note the registration number then – these crooks have quite an organization, we are beginning to realize, so it's quite likely they have access to car registration records, perhaps through a bent cop, and there you are!"

"This puts the cap on it, Alex – we have no option but to sell the Alvis, much as it might distress us to do it, poor thing!"

"And then find a successor, Mel – I quite liked the Riley we borrowed in Huddersfield that time, so that's a possibility. We shall have to ask one of our police friends whether it's possible to have a registration that suppresses the owners' details, like an ex-directory telephone number – which we should also have, come to think of it!"

Mel got dressed, they had another cup of tea, and left the flat to go to the office. The Alvis had been left in the street, not in its usual place in the mews, and when they came down the front steps they were met with an astounding sight – a fire-engine in the final stages of damping down the burnt-out wreckage of their car! There was a senior fire officer supervising his men, and Alex approached him and said, "That's our car! When did all this happen?"

"Can you tell me your name, Sir? Can you show me something to bear out what you just said?" Alex found the receipt for the car registration that he had tucked in his wallet, and this satisfied the man, who explained, "We have to be careful, Mr Crabbe, you could have been a reporter or anyone! We had an emergency call only half an hour ago, from a shop-keeper, a Mrs Pendleton, who saw someone throw something into the front seat and run off, and then the car burst into flames! My men just found an empty petrol can in the car. This appears to have been a deliberate act, Mr Crabbe! Have you any idea who did this and why? The police should be here soon."

Alex comforted Melpomene, who was openly weeping, part in grief, part in terror, he thought. Then they gave all their particulars to a policeman who had just arrived on his bike, said thanks to the firemen, who got into their engine and left after satisfying themselves there was no chance of the fire springing up again. The policeman said he would get the car, or what was left of it, taken to the police yard, saying, "We shall have to conduct a full forensic examination, though I doubt that we could find any fingerprints now – but that's up to the experts!"

Alex and Mel went back into the flat to have another cup of tea and tell Caroline all about it, just as the telephone rang.

Mel picked it up and it was Marjorie, who said, with her voice trembling, "I just had a call from a man who didn't say who he was – he was laughing in a nasty way, and he said something like 'Tell your detective friends that their car was just a warning, and they'd better pull their heads in before we have to take things further!' then he rang off – what did he mean about the car?"

Mel said, "It has been burnt out by crooks! Alex and I are perfectly all right, although we are appalled, naturally. We'll get a taxi and come over very soon, and we can have a general talk about everything. As soon as we arrive, can you get onto Jimmy Manley, please Marjorie? See you very soon!"

Chapter 39

As soon as they walked into the office, Marjorie picked up the telephone and dialled Jimmy's number. He answered straight away, so she passed the telephone to Mel. Before she had a chance to say more than her name, Jimmy said, "Yes, Mel, we heard about your car just now – these villains are getting much too uppity for my liking!"

Mel said, "But that's not all, Jimmy – Marjorie took a threatening call a few minutes ago from someone gloating over the car and promising worse! I am terribly worried – they must know both our addresses! There's not only Alex and me to consider, but Marjorie and Caroline and Mrs M too! They may even get on to our other people and contacts – Winnie is in Northampton with Stephanie Walters at the moment, so she should be safe, but who knows – I'm getting the feeling we're dealing with a hugely dangerous organization! What can we do, Jimmy – any ideas?"

"I'll let you into a secret, Mel – we are already keeping several premises and individuals under surveillance!" said Jimmy Manley, "I must admit, we missed the arsonists this morning – we had your office staked out, but not the flat – we've remedied that now! We've had a watch on Pengelly House for a while – I've got a report on my desk right now which lists everyone who has gone in and out of that house over the last few days – including a suspicious pair of gas inspectors! We have the names for some of these, but only descriptions of others. And we have somebody stationed in a house opposite the boarding-house in Limehouse which appears to be the residence of most of the Atkinson tribe, which, we've found out, includes your friend Considine, a cousin of theirs, whose real name is Kostas Apollo – no wonder he changed it!"

"Are these watchers all policemen, Jimmy? It seems like a major operation!"

"No, Mel, you're right to ask – some are regular plain-clothes police, or off-duty uniforms picking up a bit extra, but most are what we call in the trade 'snitches' or 'canaries', either petty criminals trying to keep their noses clean, or, in at least one case, an actual gang member acting as a stool-pigeon. I've been authorized to tell you and Alex that we are also under orders from the specialist art group at Scotland Yard who are working with people you know from the continent – mentioning no names! Its just me and Cec Thompson, at Mile End Road here who are in on that secret, not the rest of the station! And, finally, I am keeping in touch with your friend Detective Inspector Walters in Northampton. By the way, if you can give me the name of the shop in the Portobello Road where you found those etchings, we can send someone to see whether there is anything else to be discovered there."

"Ooh, thanks Jimmy – all this makes me feel a lot better. Now, a further question – we still have the keys to the Hampstead house with the strong-room. Should we leave it to some of your colleagues to search it, now that you are generally involved? I was looking forward to doing it ourselves, but somehow I've become less keen lately!"

"Have you got second earpieces on your new telephones?" asked Jimmy, "If so, ask Alex to listen in if he's there, as I have some information you both need to consider."

"He's been listening all along!"

"Good, here we go – Mel, you should get yourself a pistol immediately, I know you've been thinking along those lines – a Beretta wasn't it? That's a good gun for keeping in a lady's handbag, but it doesn't use the same ammunition as the Luger, so you'll have to buy your own and keep it separate. Since you've been threatened, I've asked my Super to provide you with a recommendation that you can take to the Yard, so that they will issue you with a licence straight away. Maybe they will have a Beretta at the same place that Alex got his Luger."

"I'll have to go there by taxi, of course, Jimmy," said Mel, "but I'll get onto it immediately. Can I call in at the station for the letter shortly? I won't take Alex with me, because if I do, I know what will happen! The man in the gun shop will do all the talking to him, while I stand there like an ornament!"

Jimmy laughed, "I know what you mean – I suppose garage people do the same to you when they talk about cars! As for that strong-room, I'm afraid I must disappoint you – we have already cleaned it out! We discovered that, amongst other goods, there were indeed some art works, so we have taken the contents to the Yard for the specialist squad to go through. They, of course, are not giving out any information, but you might be able to prevail on your continental friends to give you what little they might judge to be useful for tracking our gang members down."

Mel thanked him and walked to the cab-rank just down the street. She was away for nearly two hours, but reappeared with a grin on her face and something fairly heavy in her handbag, mainly the box of ammunition, because the pistol was quite light. Alex and Marjorie both admired it, Marjorie even saying she wouldn't mind having one herself, but on second thoughts, she didn't want to turn Crabbe and Crabbe into some sort of fortress!

"Once the dealer saw I was serious," said Mel, "he hardly patronized me at all – except to say 'They make quite a bang, these Berettas, small as they are!' – so I told him that I had fired a Luger, and that shut him up!"

"Right," said Alex, "the next order of business is to get ourselves a new motor – we can't go wasting time and money on taxi-rides all the time! Got any ideas, Mel? I know two or three dealers in this general area, including one for Rolls-Royce – but that's possibly a bit out of our league!"

"If there's a Riley showroom, why don't we try there? We both quite liked that one with the pre-selector gears in Huddersfield, didn't we? And I'll let you do some of the talking, if you're a good boy!"

So, less than an hour later, a black Riley four-seat tourer with the top up drew up outside the office. Marjorie came down to admire it and said, "I suppose you chose black so it wouldn't be too conspicuous, is that right?"

"That's right!" said Mel, "Go and mind the telephones, Alex, and I'll take Marjorie for a spin and explain the gear-shift to her! Look, Marjorie, it has a boot, too, so we won't be carrying stuff in a Dicky-seat any more!"

But this reminded her of the Alvis, so she had to blow her nose and wipe one or two tears from her eyes, before Marjorie jumped in and was taken for a local tour.

When they got back in the office, Mel said, "I think I spotted the watcher outside, Alex! He was standing in a doorway and said nothing, but when he caught me looking, he winked! That makes me feel better. He had a good look at the Riley, too. I forgot to ask Jimmy about anonymous registration, so we must look into that soon."

Chapter 40

Melpomene rang Jimmy to ask about registration, "Jimmy, sorry to keep bothering you! We just picked up our new car – a Riley tourer, black, which shouldn't be as easy to spot as the Alvis. I wonder if we could register it so that rogues are prevented from finding out our address from the number – can this be done legally? We don't want to give a fictitious name and address, since we're fairly law-abiding citizens! By the way, I've now got a nice little Beretta – maybe I can come to your station for a bit of a practice some time. The cocking and safety arrangements are not the same as on the Luger."

"Certainly, Mel! Do you want to come now – I'm not doing anything urgent at the moment?"

"Right, see you in a flash, Jimmy – I'll get Alex to come too."

They parked in the yard at Mile End Road – the young policemen on the gate recognized them, remarked on the new car, and pointed out a shed where two men in white coats could be seen raking over the remains of the Alvis – Melpomene turned away, shuddering.

Jimmy took them to the firing range, saw Mel loose off a few rounds, then declared himself satisfied, "Good grouping again, Mel – but you should realise that the Beretta round doesn't have the same stopping power as the Parabellum in the Luger, so maybe a shot to a villain's leg won't produce the same instant effect as you have been used to! I'm not saying 'shoot to kill', but a shoulder shot might be worth trying! Now, let's go up to my office, I've got a couple of things to tell you."

DC Cec Thompson produced some decent cups of tea without needing to be asked, and even had some jam tarts to offer!

"First," said Jimmy, "I've made some enquiries with the car registration people, and they say that they can record an entry that states, 'Owner's details unavailable – make application to Head Office'. That would satisfy your requirements! Tell me the number now, and I'll ask them to fix it right away."

"Oh, thank you, Jimmy," said Mel, "you are always such a help!"

"It's no bother to us – we get a lot from you in return, you know! Now, Mrs Ida Pendleton, the shopkeeper who called the fire brigade when she saw your Alvis being torched, says she got a good look at the two men who did it, and was able to give us detailed descriptions. One of them sported a walrus moustache, like Francis Atkinson, and the description of the other fits Terence Forbes, so they could be the same pair who menaced you with knives at Hampstead. They were working together then, so they are probably regular partners."

Mel clapped her hands to her cheeks, "Oh-oh! We were supposed to come and identify them, but with so much going on, we forgot! Did you have to let them go?"

"I'm afraid we did – we just didn't have enough evidence to hold them without yours – but not to worry, Mel, we can fix that omission right now! Since both of them are known to you, I have worked out a plan. I told you before that we've been watching the boarding-house in Limehouse where most of the Atkinson clan hang out. We can't burst in and make arrests until we have something definite to go on – in the view of the courts we only have hearsay evidence so far. There are eight or nine sets of rooms in the boarding-house, so we can't just blunder in without knowing who to look for, and where. The gang relies on this – I expect there are ordinary tenants there who are tolerated by the villains for this very reason – but what they don't know is that the ground-floor flat by the front door, not popular because it's noisy, has been rented by the Metropolitan Police for over a month. Today the residents will be a couple of policemen and Mr and Mrs Crabbe! So, bring your books and crossword puzzles and settle down for a wait that could be quite long!"

"So what are we waiting for and what do we do?" asked Alex.

"When you hear someone coming up or down the front steps you can look through the spyhole on your front door and see if you recognize them. When you do, your room-mates can pounce! Apart from the two arsonists, you might spot the illustrious Countess Wybrowska, or even Keith Satterfield or his pals from the auction ring!"

"Right, Jimmy, when do we go?" asked Melpomene, "Have we got time to go back to our flat? I need The Times, for the crossword, and although I have my pistol, I think Alex would like his, too. Who knows what might happen?"

"Quite right, Mel, and I'll pick up my copy of the latest Dr Thorndyke novel by Austin Freeman, 'Helen Vardon's Confession' that I've just borrowed from the library, to get me into the right frame of mind!"

"So please come back here when you have everything," said Jimmy, "and we'll see about getting you disguised and smuggled into position!"

So, an hour later, with the watcher in the opposite house signalling that all was clear, a nun, accompanied by three Catholic priests in black soutanes, could have been observed entering the ground-floor apartment of Limehouse Mansions, each of them carrying a small battered cardboard suitcase.

Once inside, Melpomene discarded her veil and wimple, putting them aside so that she could replace them quickly if necessary, while the priests kept their soutanes on.

Everyone opened their little suitcases, Mel and Alex getting stuck into their crossword or book, while Detective Constable Frank Watts took out the form page of the 'Pink 'Un' and started planning his wagers for the Saturday meeting at Kempton Park, and his companion, DC Phil Fellows, continued studying the manuals in preparation for his application for promotion to Sergeant.

Nothing happened for nearly two hours, and then they all heard heavy footsteps coming up to the front door. Mel rushed to apply her eye to the peephole, holding her hand up to the others for 'hush', but then stood back, saying, "Only a parcel being delivered."

Then Alex said, "This might be an opportunity to get a peep into one of the flats. I'll take my Bible and wander after the delivery man. If anyone asks me I'll say I'm looking for Mrs Braithwaite."

He opened the door to the hallway, peering after the man to make sure no one else was around, then stepped out, head down, apparently studying the Good Book. The delivery man was looking at the panel of doorbells, muttering under his breath, "Dawkins, Dawkins, there ain't no Dawkins!" Then he squared his shoulders and went to the closest door on that floor, knocked and it was opened. Alex couldn't see who was there, but a woman's voice said, "Yes?" and the man said, "I've got a package for Dawkins, which flat would that be?"

Chapter 41

The woman said politely, "I'm sorry, I don't know a Dawkins – are you sure that's what it says?" She stepped out and they both looked closely at the parcel, and the man shook his head and said, "Yus, it's Dawkins all right, I shall just have to take it back to the depot. This is Limehouse Mansions, isn't it?"

He turned to leave, and Alex approached the woman and said, in an ingratiating tone, "While you are at the door, my dear, I wonder if I could trouble you a little more. I am looking for a Mrs Braithwaite – I hope I shall be more successful than our friend there. I think I have the name right – she is a lady of middle age – perhaps you know of a neighbour I might try?"

"Well no, Father, the only women I know in this building are the Countess, on the second floor and Mrs Dierdre Atkinson on the third. There's also another Mrs Atkinson, but she's very elderly – she lives here on the ground floor at the back, with her two adult sons, but they are hardly ever at home – the Lord knows what they do – oh, sorry, Father."

"Thank you anyway, my dear, and God bless you!" said Alex, and went back to the flat, the woman having closed her door.

When Alex went back, he said, "I think I may have missed my vocation, Brothers and Sister! Sorry, I shouldn't mock! I did find out that our friend the Countess is on the second floor, and two Mrs Atkinsons as well, on this floor and the third. And a couple of male Atkinsons on this floor, too – but you police might know all this already!"

"No, we didn't!" said Frank, "We could go and grab the Countess now – you two have enough on her already to make an arrest stick!"

But his colleague, Phil Fellows was more cautious, "We'd better check with Jimmy, first," he said, "let's give him a call!"

Mel and Alex looked around and couldn't see a telephone, so Phil, with a grin, opened a wardrobe door to disclose one within, with a dial, even!

Jimmy asked, "Do you know the actual flat, or just the floor?" and Phil asked Alex in turn, who said, "No, but I can do my Mrs Braithwaite bit, that seemed to go down well!" So Jimmy agreed, but warned they should be very cautious, "Let Phil and Alex go to the flats, but have Frank and Mel waiting round the corner, or by the stairs, whatever seems best! Don't forget your pistols, but it won't be easy to draw them, the way you're dressed. We should have thought of this!"

Mel thought for a moment and then said, "You know how nuns often modestly keep their arms folded in front of them – let's see!"

She grasped her Beretta in her right hand, crossed her arms with her hands joined and then shook her full sleeves down so they covered hands and weapon, "How's that!" she exclaimed triumphantly, "And if I need to, I can take my left hand out and keep the other sleeve down!"

Alex and DC Fellowes climbed the stairs to the second floor and saw that there were only two doors there. Alex made sure his glasses – a disguise device – were in place and knocked on the nearest door. Mel and Frank were waiting on the landing, out of sight.

A short woman who Alex didn't recognize opened the door and asked, curtly at first, "Yes, what do you want. Oh, sorry, Father, I didn't see it was a priest. Can I help at all?"

"Perhaps, my daughter – I am looking for Countess Wybrowska, is this the right place?"

"Yes, Father – I'll see if she's in. Please step inside." Alex went in, motioning Phil Fellowes to stay outside. The woman called out "Doreen! A visitor for you!", at which there was a clatter from an inner room and a muffled shriek, followed by the sound of rapid footsteps as the Countess rushed out of the second door into the corridor and ran past Phil, who made an ineffectual grab at her that she evaded.

She ran for the stairs and was seized by Frank, while Mel levelled her gun at her. Phil joined them, and the fugitive was soon hand-cuffed! Phil then said, "Doreen May Atkinson, I am arresting you for a number of offences including fraud. You will be charged at the police station with these. You do not have to say anything, but it may harm your defence if you do not mention when questioned something which you later rely on in court. Anything you do say may be given in evidence!"

While all this was happening, Alex, hearing the commotion, turned to leave, and saw that the woman who had answered the door had picked up the telephone. She said only "Look out, Mr Banfield, we're being raided ..." before Alex pressed down the telephone hook and cut her off. He grasped her arm and took her outside, where Frank took over and both captives were led down to the ground-floor flat.

Jimmy was telephoned and arrived outside in his car, along with a Black Maria, which took the criminals away. He said, "I don't know what we'll get the second woman for, but aiding and abetting will be enough for now. Let's move away a bit and see whether her warning has had any effect!"

The two policemen had gone off in the van with the prisoners, so Alex and Mel joined Jimmy in his unmarked car a few yards up the street to await developments. Jimmy said, "You had better take out your Luger, Alex, just in case. I see that Mel is already brandishing her pistol!"

It was only ten or fifteen minutes later that two big black saloon cars stopped outside the flats with a squeal of brakes. Three huge bruisers leapt out of the first and took up defensive positions along the front of the building, with their right hands in their side pockets, while a uniformed chauffeur got out of the second car, went round and opened the rear door.

The thug nearest that car looked around and nodded, whereupon the chauffeur handed out an elegantly-dressed gentleman in, perhaps, his late fifties, with neat greying hair and a closely trimmed beard. They both went into the boarding-house.

Alex, of course, was writing down the numbers of both cars.

Jimmy said, "Do either of you recognize him – I don't! We certainly have nothing that would let us detain him – someone like that probably has tame lawyers on tap anyway. What a pity none of us has a camera – all we can do is try to fix his description in our memories. I'll check with our watcher across the street to see whether he has shown up before. We can't possibly go in there now, with all those goons watching out!"

"The woman used the name 'Banfield' on the telephone," said Alex, "but they all probably use aliases as a matter of course, so that might not help, either."

"Never mind!" said Jimmy, "Everything comes to he who waits – and we've got a couple of them to show for our efforts today, as well as a little more information about the residents there."

Chapter 42

Alex said, "I'm quite puzzled! When the woman rang, she said they were being raided. Now I would have expected that such a warning would make them keep their heads down, or even retreat to some safe place, but what happens? This grand person turns up! He is obviously a big wheel in the organization, judging by the cars and his henchmen, so why would he risk being spotted?"

"I've been thinking along these lines, too," said Melpomene, "and one thought that enters my head is that he feels invulnerable – meaning that either he is an out-and-out megalomaniac, or believes he has support in high places! You will recall, Alex, that our continental friend suspected that there had been infiltration into the forces of law and order by elements of certain criminal organizations. I'm sorry, Jimmy, if I'm sounding somewhat obscure, but we are committed to confidentiality in these matters!"

"All we can do, I think," said Jimmy, "is wait and watch. The cars arrived only ten or fifteen minutes after Alex cut off the warning call, so their headquarters can't be very far from here. I feel reluctant to follow them when they set off again, but we can at least note which direction they go. Once we're back in the station we can look up those car numbers – not that they will tell us much – these people seem to cover their tracks thoroughly – except for today, apparently!"

Mel had another thought, "This district is rather run-down, even slummy – I can't think that our elegant friend would choose to live in such surroundings – even though Dr Fu Manchu was supposed to have his headquarters in an opium-den here – are there any better-class areas close by, Jimmy?"

"Let me think – as you say, Limehouse is not the most salubrious address! But between here and my Mile End Road police station, especially if you veer off towards Stepney, there are one or two more respectable residential areas that might suit him. Look out – here he comes! We might follow them at a discreet distance."

The elegant man and all his entourage got back into their motors, but instead of just driving ahead, they all did a sharp u-turn and headed off the way they had come. By the time Jimmy had turned his car, the crooks had vanished. Jimmy drove that way, but there was soon a cross-roads, so he gave up and took everyone back to the station.

He got Cec Thompson to check on the car registrations, but after he had talked on the telephone a while, he turned back to them, saying, with a grin, "Owner's details unavailable – make application to Head Office!"

"Well, do so then, Constable!" said Jimmy, not really annoyed, "Tell them who you are and they will cooperate. You may have to give them your warrant-card number."

Cec spent a few more minutes on the telephone and then the others heard him groan, as he hung up and said, "You wouldn't credit this – they are both registered to a Mr Robinson at – wait for it – 'Pengelly House ...'"

The others chimed in, "... Fairford Avenue, Wimbledon!"

"That does it!" said Jimmy, "I'm going to apply for a search warrant for Pengelly House, and descend on the place with a squad of uniforms and do it over from cellar to attic! Enough is enough! I'd invite you along for the ride, Mel and Alex, but I think it would be better for you to keep away for the moment. Some of them know you already, but not all!"

Mel and Alex changed back out of their religious garb and set off back to the office, thanking Jimmy for the entertaining interlude. It was nearly 5.30, so Mel gave an account of the day to Marjorie and said, "One more phone call and I'm calling it a day! Tell me Jens-Olle's number – can I dial him direct or do I have to go through the exchange?"

"Well, before we had dials, we had to ask the exchange for an overseas line, so I guess you'll still need to do this – so just dial '0'."

Mel did so, while Alex listened on the other earpiece, and after a wait of only a few minutes, got her connection. "Hello, Jens-Olle, Melpomene here – what mischief have you been up to? No, don't tell me now, I want to ask you something first – have you come across the name 'Banfield'?"

She went on to explain the circumstances, and then Jens-Olle said, "You really saw this man? This is excellent news! I will tell you a bit about him. I told you that we suspected leaks in the police organization, and this man – his full name is Edwin

McCauley Banfield – is involved at a high level! He was married for some years to the sister of a District Commissioner of the Danish Police Force – this is the equivalent of the British rank of Chief Superintendent – and divorced her two years ago when he discovered that she was a cocaine addict. He threatened to disclose this to the press, which accounts for the hold he has over the District Commissioner, who would be forced to resign if anything came out. The Danes are an extremely puritanical race! And I suppose that high levels in the British police have been asked to keep away too, for alleged 'diplomatic reasons'. But any such edicts are unlikely to have spread down to station levels, so if you warn your Detective-Sergeant about all this, he should still have enough authority to take certain actions without bothering the upper levels of the hierarchy."

"You wouldn't happen to have an address for Banfield, would you, Jens-Olle? We weren't able to pursue him today, but we believe we know the general area."

"I will check for you, Melpomene. Our bureau staff have left for the day, but I will get onto it first thing in the morning! By the way, I have heard from young Mortensen – he tells me he has started working with your Inspector Walters and Miss Morris in Northampton, and that they have already filled a few gaps in the files, in particular they have located some of the associates of your famous Mr Postlethwaite – did I pronounce it well this time? Maybe you could ring them tomorrow, you've probably done enough for one day! Godnat, Frøken Melpomene!"

"What do you think of all that, Alex?" said Mel happily, "It sounds as though we might be getting somewhere at last! Goodnight, Marjorie, see you in the morning! How are your hands, are they a hundred percent now?"

"Yes, thank you, Mel – I still get a twinge now and then, but less and less as time goes on. I'm riding my bike again now – I was a bit leery of it for a few days, but now I'm fine! Good night!"

They drove back to the flat, Mel at the wheel, and put the Riley safely into the mews garage, locking it carefully.

Then they went indoors and were greeted by the delicious aroma of something Italian, which Mrs M told them was her version of 'rice otter á la milliners', which Mel thought might be Risotto alla Milanese. She found she had guessed right!

Chapter 43

While Mel and Alex were at breakfast, the telephone rang and Mel answered – it was Marjorie, "I just had a call from Jens-Olle Pedersen – he has apparently decided that I am to be trusted with information now! Here is the address of Mr Banfield, have you got something to write it down? Cuckoo Cottage, Stepney Park – doesn't sound like a place where a big-wig would live, does it! He also says I should remind you to call Stephanie or Winnie, and he gave me Niels Mortensen's number, too – or his landlady's really."

Mel told Alex about Banfield's address. "We should let Jimmy know straight away," she said, "and he can send Cec or another plain-clothes policeman to check it out. I'll telephone him now."

But when someone at the station answered it was to say, "You've missed DS Manley and DC Thomson, I'm afraid, Mrs Crabbe, they've set off with a van-load of police – to Wimbledon, they said. It's a pity you weren't here to see them – they'd dug out their uniforms – Jimmy's looked a bit snug around the stomach – and they were both trailing the scent of moth-balls!"

"Thanks! Could you ask Jimmy to telephone us at the office when he gets back, please"

"Certainly, Mrs Crabbe, but I'm pretty sure he won't need to be reminded!"

Mel told Alex that the Wimbledon operation was under way, saying, "Next we'll ring Northampton and see what they've been getting up to! But let's do it from the office, OK?"

As they went into the mews to collect the car, an idler standing smoking at the corner winked at them, and gave a slight nod of the head. Mel smiled back and they got the car out of the garage and drove to the office.

As they went into the main office, Marjorie was on the telephone – she waved them a greeting and after a few more minutes' conversation, rang off.

"I don't know!" she said, "The more work we have the more approaches from new clients we're getting! That was a lady with a rather upper-class accent, who sounded as though she had a case that would appeal to us! She wouldn't give me all the details – she gave her number, which sounded fairly local – London, anyway – and asked whether 'one of the professionals' could call her back at their convenience. She did say that it concerned a burglary, but a very puzzling one, that involved some valuable Japanese prints."

"Thanks, Marjorie!" said Melpomene, "We'll get onto that after we've spoken to Northampton. Can you get Winnie for us, please?"

It was Stephanie who answered, "We're all three of us here this morning, Melpomene, preparing a big report to send to Jens-Olle, with copies to Hugo Palance and to our contact at Scotland Yard, whose name we've been given permission to pass on to you – he is Deputy Commissioner Sir Adrian Fitz-Hugh. He has been involved in the art project since the beginning."

"That sounds very promising, Stephanie, so you and the others have been making progress, I assume. Can you give us a brief run-down? – Alex is listening, too."

"First, we have got definite locations of almost all of the ones who were plotting at the Hendersons' dinner party, even the elusive Postlethwaite! Messrs Perkins and Benson were straightforward, they had never made any attempt at concealment, and were still carrying on their occupations in the town, but William Satterfield and 'Fido' Barker took more work. As for the ones that you caught at the auction, Melpomene – as you know they were released on bail, so the uniform branch were able to find Winton and Wilmot and serve notices to them to appear in court, which will happen next week, I believe, while Liversedge is tied up with the Atkinson clan. We know nothing up here about the second Satterfield, Keith – maybe he is also with the Atkinsons?"

Stephanie went on, "Apparently you haven't seen the papers yet this morning. We only just got the London papers up here – I get two or three every day. If you've got The Times, you might be interested in a story on page two!"

"Hang on!" said Mel, "Alex is just looking – and he appears to have found the one you're referring to. Read it out, Alex – they've already seen it! I'll get back to you in a while, Stephanie, meanwhile give my love to Winnie and my regards to Niels, and say we hope to meet him in the flesh soon!"

Alex read out, in a dramatic tone, "*GHASTLY MASSACRE IN LIMEHOUSE TENEMENT. Philip Dixon, Bureau Chief. Yesterday evening, a distraught woman telephoned the Putney Police Station from an apartment in a boarding-house, in an incoherent state. After the police had arrived and she had been calmed down she related the following macabre story. 'I was visiting my old Auntie, what lives in the boarding-house. She's been a bit sick, and hadn't been able to go out to the shops. I wanted to make her a cup of tea, but there weren't any milk, so I told her I would pop next door and borrow some. I knocked on the door, but nobody answered, so I was about to give up when I noticed the door was ajar. I pushed it open and called out, but there was no reply. And then I heard horrible groaning! I went in, thinking someone needed help, and in the front room I saw this woman, still groaning, face down on a settee, with a knife a-sticking out of her back! I couldn't hardly credit my eyes! I didn't dare pull the knife out, so I started to look around to find something to staunch the bleeding, and in the next room, what did I see but three more dead people, two men and a woman, all lying in great pools of blood! I don't mind telling you, I panicked and ran out back into my auntie's place. She's had the telephone put on, so's she can get help if she takes a turn – she hasn't been well for ages! So I rang the police and they arrived very quickly, bless 'em. They called the ambulance and the undertaker, while I sat with auntie having cups of tea – they'd found us some milk next door, because she wouldn't be needing it no more!'*

On arrival, having settled down and questioned their informant, the police made a thorough search of the building, but could find no further evidence of any wrong-doing. The apartment concerned has been sealed. More in our later editions as further information comes to hand."

Mel turned to the others and said, "I'm feeling rather glad we didn't tangle with those people yesterday afternoon, pistols or no pistols! What a pity Jimmy was out this morning, that has cost us a few hours, which might have made all the difference. Now all we can do is wait and bite our nails!"

"I've never observed you doing that, Mel!" said Alex, "You are too contained for that, as long as you are kept supplied with tea. Would you like a cup now?"

"Oh, yes please – have we got any jam tarts, Marjorie?"

Chapter 44

Melpomene rang Stephanie again, saying, "Yesterday, Alex and I took the cloth, so to speak, as priest and nun respectively, and conducted a foray into the Atkinson boarding-house in Limehouse, where we and a couple of Jimmy's men nabbed the Countess Wybrowska, otherwise Doreen Atkinson, and another woman. This activity tempted a certain Mr Edwin McCauley Banfield, well-known to Jens-Olle already, to emerge from the woodwork and visit the flats with a bunch of his goons. What he did there, we didn't know until we read The Times article you told us about! To add to all this, Jens-Olle has found for us the home address of this man, who has every sign of being a senior figure in the criminal hierarchy. Finally, car registration records revealed that he uses Pengelly House as the registered address of two of his cars, so there might be more connections to be picked up from that."

"Now we have some further news for you!" said Mel, "Our redoubtable Detective Sergeant Jimmy Manley is at this very moment conducting an assault on Pengelly House. When Alex and I were inspecting the gas systems in that place, we came across Keith Satterfield and the mysterious Eliza Stanford, as well as Liversedge and Wilmot, who are both in one way or another involved in the auction ring industry. There were others at the meeting that was going on at the time, who we didn't recognize. Just who Jimmy and his band will scoop up in the current exercise, we don't yet know. It's possible that, apart from people, they will come across other evidence, even some artworks – we shall see!"

She rang off, and after everyone had finished talking, Mel said, "We'd better let someone at Mile End Road know about Banfield's address. If they move fast enough, they have a chance of catching him before he goes to ground, but he could have already disappeared, they seem to be very resourceful!" She had been dialling as she spoke, and recognised the voice who answered as the one she had spoken to before.

"Melpomene Crabbe here again! No doubt all of you at the station have heard about this Limehouse massacre – well we have evidence that a Mr Banfield was involved! Jimmy, my husband Alex and I saw him arrive with his heavies yesterday afternoon. I tried to let Jimmy know the address we had been given for this guy this morning, but he'd already set out for Wimbledon. So please make sure that those involved in following up this incident are told that Mr Edwin McCauley Banfield was at the scene yesterday afternoon, and that his address is Cuckoo Cottage, Stepney Park. Have you got all that?"

"Certainly have, Mrs Crabbe, I'll get on to it straight away, and thank you very much!"

"Lunchtime, I think!" declared Alex, "We need an interlude out of the office to clear our heads. What about a counter lunch at 'The Five Bells' – we haven't done that for ages! Possibly not since we were students! We'll only be an hour Marjorie – did you bring your sandwiches again or shall we bring you back a pork pie or something?"

"No thanks, Alex – my Mum made me up a lovely egg salad! Don't rush back, I can hold the fort – but do you want to ring the Japanese prints lady before you go?"

"Good thought, Marjorie – we mustn't forget to keep our prospective clients happy! Please ring her for me, and we'll see what it is all about."

When Alex spoke to the woman, Mrs Halliwell by name, she was on her way out of her house, so Alex suggested that she should come to the office later in the afternoon and discuss her case with both of them, to which she countered that it would suit her a lot better if they could come to her house, with an address in a secluded square near Finsbury Park, since she wished to show them her entire collection – or what was left of it!

So, after a gentle stroll back from the pub, where they had partaken of an enjoyable lunch, Melpomene and Alex drove to Finsbury Park and parked outside a Georgian house in a terrace of similar, well kept-up houses with gleaming brass door fittings and pristine white-painted window frames and doors.

They rang the bell and were admitted by a smartly-dressed maid, who showed them into an elegant drawing-room, with paintings, etchings and prints of a variety of styles almost filling the wall space over a rich wine-coloured wallpaper. In a few minutes, Mrs Halliwell swept in. Surprisingly, she seemed no older than Melpomene and was dressed in riding clothes, including breeches and a tweed hacking jacket.

She led them up the first flight of a sweeping staircase and into a long room, almost a gallery, whose walls were the setting for an carefully arranged sequence of prints which were clearly based on a historical theme, completely made up of Japanese wood-block prints.

"I am indebted to my dear departed Mama for these treasures," she explained proudly, "I have only quite recently had the wherewithal to start adding to them. She collected them over many years travelling in the East, with her father, my grandfather, who held various posts in the diplomatic service."

"And now," said Mrs Halliwell, "let me turn to the reason why I approached your agency. I have recently become aware of certain subtle mismatches that have crept into the collection. Let me show you an example."

She led them to a print depicting a landscape of conifer woods and stony crags, done in monochrome but with a few highlights picked out in a metallic foil.

"Now, unless you are a true connoisseur – and I do not count myself among that number – you might not see anything exceptional in this print. I would not have noticed anything myself, until I recalled a feature of this work that had caught my fancy when I first acquired it, namely that this tree just here had an outline which resembled the head of a horse. No, there is no use squinting at it now, this is simply not the same tree!"

"You mean that it has been switched?" asked Alex, "That this is not the print that you remembered?"

"Precisely!" she said, "To cut a long story short, this started me examining those few prints that I had purchased myself, First I simply looked at them, and than, one day, almost on a whim, I took one carefully out of its frame. And on the back – look and I will show you – I discovered a hand-written letter. Read what this one says, please!"

Alex peered closely at a few sentences in a crabbed hand, possibly written with a quill pen, which said, "Many thanks for my print, once again in my possession. Here is a work of equivalent value, which I wish you to receive in recompense. Fair exchange is no robbery. If you disagree, dear lady, I deeply regret that, but I cannot let you have what is rightfully mine!"

Chapter 45

Alex said, "This is very strange, Mrs Halliwell! You have of course no idea who can have done this, or you would not have put your problem to us in those terms. When did you first notice the substitution?"

"No more than a month ago, Mr Crabbe, but I have no way of knowing when the switch was made. I have owned this particular print for over two years, and the others which have been meddled with for as long ago as five. I can date this quite well, because I inherited a sum of money then which allowed me to indulge this particular passion of mine – I have others, as perhaps you might have noticed! By the way, please call me Miranda – may I also use your first names?"

"Of course, Miranda!" said Melpomene, "He is Alex, and I am Melpomene – in a while, you might feel like calling me Mel! Can I ask a further question? Is it only the prints that you purchased yourself, or are there any of those in your Mother's collection that have been affected?"

"I wondered about this, Melpomene – what an euphonious name! – but I was unwilling to take off the frames or the backing paper. I have thought of seeking the help of a skilled conservator for this task – what do you think?"

"We have worked with a woman conservator, Alexandra Mainwaring – would you like us to approach her on this matter?" replied Mel, "Apart from that, we would need to find out more about Japanese prints – can you recommend some experts?"

"Please do talk to your conservator for me, that would be very helpful. As for experts, allow me to think about this for a while. I am becoming quite hopeful that together we shall be able to find answers to this mystery! We must discuss terms when next we meet. Thank you both!"

On the way back to the office, Mel said, "We must not get too far ahead of ourselves, Alex. I will not be able to direct my full attention onto this case until we have cleared up most of the other. I don't feel that this one has anything to do with our main case – what do you think?"

"I agree with you on both points, Mel. Until we get evidence to the contrary we should regard the two as separate, and certainly avoid rushing into Miranda Halliwell's case too precipitously!"

"Meanwhile," added Mel, "I'm all agog to hear if Jimmy has any developments to report!"

And, as soon as they entered the office, they found Marjorie in an excited state, "Jimmy is back at the station!" she announced, "He says he has plenty to report – but he wouldn't let on to me, the beast! You're to telephone him the instant you get back!"

She was already dialling, and Alex went to the phone, while Mel took the second earpiece this time.

"Hello Mel and Alex – two different reports for you!" said Jimmy, "First I must tell you we had mixed results at Pengelly House. We came away with three people in the Black Maria, sent two off in an ambulance and saw the dust of two more escaping so quickly in a car that we had no chance of catching them! When I've given you all those details, I'll tell you about Banfield! You'll have to contain yourselves for a few moments, I'm afraid!"

"Ok, Jimmy, fire away, we're both sitting comfortably!" said Alex, "And we are both listening!"

"I'll tell you about the ambulance patients, first. The enigmatic Eliza Stanford was the first to succumb – we did not wait to be invited in, but burst open the front doors and rushed inside, and saw that she was walking down the front stairs. When she saw me and my squad she fainted, I think – in any case she tumbled down the rest of the stairs and finished up in a heap. One of my men – we all have St John's Ambulance Certificates, of course – rushed to her aid and found she had regained consciousness but had her leg twisted underneath her with what he thought was a sprained ankle. So we rang for the ambulance, while a maid was called to tend to the invalid, who had been helped to a couch in the entrance hall. Score: 1!"

"All this, of course, caused a certain amount of commotion, and I divided our forces into two groups. Cec took three to search the downstairs rooms, and I and the others went up the staircase to the dining-room, where you had found the meeting going on when you were being gas inspectors. As we got to the landing, a bunch of them came streaming out, and one of them,

137

who we found out later was Keith Satterfield, was misguided enough to draw a revolver on us. PC Malone, who has a mantelpiece full of medals he won at Bisley competitions over the last three years, dropped him with a shot to the shoulder, causing him to let go of his weapon – remember that, Mel! This somewhat perturbed the rest of the bunch, and we had no difficulty persuading them to come with us down the stairs for interrogation."

" 'Persuading' sounds like a word you would use in court, Jimmy!" said Alex, "I hope you and your boys were not too rough!"

"How could you suggest anything like that, Alex! When the ambulance arrived, we packed Mrs Stanford and Keith Satterfield, who had been patched up with a sling by the ambulance attendant, off in it, with a constable in charge of them. Score: 2!"

"We were able to identify only three of the remaining people – they all gave false names, as you might expect, but fortunately I was able to recognize Martin Wilmot and Henry Winton, who we held after the auction ring and released on bail. And the last was the remaining Satterfield, William, who betrayed himself by addressing Keith as 'Brother' when he was comforting him just after he was shot. Score: 5!"

"So who were the two who escaped by car, Jimmy?" asked Alex.

"Hold your horses – I shall get there! And we encountered them later, as you will hear! We were forced to let the unidentified people go, since we had no evidence that anything illegal had been going on before we arrived. We did take their details, such as they were, before they went."

"Then Cec and his companions came back to report that they had startled a couple in a back room on this floor. When they saw Cec they jumped up and fled into the garden through some French windows. Cec and his pair gave chase, but the two went though a gate in the back wall and slammed it behind them. Our blokes found that there was a laneway at the back and the two crims jumped into a big black car and sped off! Cec saw the number, which he realised belonged to one of the cars involved in the Limehouse massacre. These numbers had been circulated to all stations in the general area, fortunately. So thus ended the adventure of Pengelly House!"

Chapter 46

"Not a bad story, so far!" said Melpomene, "Did you know who it was who escaped out the back?"

"There's a good chance it was Banfield and his partner in murder!" said Jimmy, "Cec told me later, as we were driving back to the station, that one of them was smart, with grey hair and a beard, and the other was wearing a chauffeur's uniform. So we drove to Cuckoo Cottage and parked a hundred yards along the street, at a place where my colleague, Sergeant Alf Stone, had stationed an observer, as soon as he had learned that address from you earlier today. This officer told me that he had seen nothing all day, so we concluded that we had guessed wrongly that Banfield was heading home. But, just as were going to give up and go back to the station, a black car passed us and turned in at the gates of the cottage, with the chauffeur driving and Banfield on board. We thought that it would be foolhardy, to say the least, for two or three of us to attempt an onslaught on the cottage – which, by the way, is really a grand mansion, belying its name, and might have had a large staff – so we made our way back to a police telephone box, rang the station and called for reinforcements in a hurry! Within twenty minutes or so, vanloads started arriving, parking down a side road not far from the cottage. Someone had had the sense to bring a megaphone, so Cec and I proceeded toward the front door, sending a detachment round to the back of the house, not wanting to be caught the same way twice! We didn't wait to ring the bell, but barged the front door open and shouted 'Police – come out with your hands up!' through the megaphone. Nothing happened at first and then, from a room off the entrance hall, we heard what sounded like maniacal laughter, making my blood run cold! And then there was a single gun-shot! I drew my own pistol, as did Cec, and we stood back and kicked the door open before cautiously entering the room, ready to take evasive action if necessary."

"That was a brave act!" said Melpomene, "But I don't know what else you could have done!"

"Yes, my thoughts were all in a whirl, but I was absolutely determined that Banfield would not escape this time! As it turned out, we had nothing to worry about. There was Banfield, weeping profusely, standing over the body of his chauffeur, with his gun in one hand and a glass in the other. He was swaying slightly, overcome either with emotion or drink! As we fund out, once we had disarmed him and put on the handcuffs, it was the latter! He was in no state to be questioned, so we cautioned him, put him in a van and took him away!"

"I sent a couple of constables to search the rest of the house, warning them to be cautious – but I reckoned that we had already dealt with the only man that posed any threat. They found almost all the staff – twelve or so all told – gathered in the kitchen and chattering excitedly, except for two or three young maids who were huddled together crying. We took their particulars and statements, of course, starting with the butler and cook-housekeeper, but I doubt whether any of them knew of the nefarious activities of their master. We sent them all away, noting their addresses for later – one or two said that they would stay with friends, as they came from fairly distant parts – and we left several policemen guarding the house until forensics and general searches could be done. The dead chauffeur was taken to the morgue for autopsy, though the cause of death was fairly obvious – a bullet-wound to the centre of the forehead!"

Alex said, "Whether or not this gentleman is involved in any criminal art organizations, he is certainly turning out to be homicidal! Have you found out the identities of the people slaughtered at Limehouse yet?"

"Not so far!" said Jimmy, "And I think I can afford to wait quite a while. In fact, I might take my family off to the country for a week to get over all this excitement! If you want to keep up with the saga, Cec Thompson is your man. He knows as much as I and has the details of all my contacts."

"You and your wife and children must be our guests, then," said Melpomene, "my family has a very nice hotel in Woodhampton in Hampshire – you could all relax there, and the food is quite passable! What do you say? Please accept it as a token of our thanks, Jimmy!"

"That's extremely nice of you, Mel, I'll talk to my wife, and we'll ring you up in a little while. Thanks a lot!"

Jimmy rang off, and Mel and Alex turned toward Marjorie. "I know – cups of tea!" she said, hastening toward the kettle, already singing on the gas-ring, "And we'll have to ask the telephone people if we can have an additional earpiece for each telephone, as well as the existing two – I could see from your faces that you were being told an exciting tale!"

"Don't worry, Marjorie!" said Melpomene, "We'll tell you the whole story – besides I am going to ring Winnie and the others right away, so you can listen as I tell them!"

Once Mel had drunk her first cup, she rang the Northampton flat, finding all three still there.

"We're just tidying up our report," said Winnie, "should we send you a copy? It might be the fourth carbon, and a little faint, but still readable – we're saving the best for Jens-Olle and the second and third for Hugo and the Scotland Yard man, Sir Adrian Fitz-Hugh."

"Don't send it, Winnie, we shall drive up to see you tomorrow, hoping that Niels Mortensen will still be with you, so you can take us through your report then. Now, if you are ready for it, I shall relate an interesting account called 'The Adventures of dauntless Jimmy Manley and his redoubtable crew at Pengelly House and Cuckoo Cottage', which you will have to relay to your companions. I suppose we shall have telephones with loudspeakers one day, with any luck!"

When Mel had finished, and answered some supplementary questions, Stephanie said, "You can add Luke Postlethwaite to your list of those in the slammer! The full story is in our report, of course, but the short version is that the foolish man turned up at the Henderson house yesterday morning – was it only yesterday, Winnie? – and tried to persuade Mildred to give him an affidavit that he had only been joking when he cast aspersions on Daphnis and Chloe. Of course, he picked the wrong woman for this! Mildred cleverly led him on and on until he blurted out the truth – that he had been put up to the whole thing by a powerful man – no name mentioned – and that if she refused to comply, harm to her might result."

"So, as soon as he left, Mildred rang the local station and told them all, with the result that friend Luke was picked up and charged with threatening behaviour intended to produce an unlawful outcome. So there remains Barker – when you come up tomorrow, Mel must bring those etchings with her – if my colleagues in forensics don't find Fido's paw-prints on one or more of them, I shall be most surprised. If you've ever tried to clean the glass or frame of a picture, you'll know what I mean!"

Chapter 47

As they were getting ready to set out for Northampton the next morning, Alex said, "Have you had any more thoughts about Miranda Halliwell's enquiry? We shouldn't leave her in suspense for too long."

"Actually, Alex, I thought we might put Sandy Mainwaring in touch with Miranda, so she can explain the situation first hand. I'll ring Sandy now and prepare her."

Mel had a chat with Anatole when he answered the phone, and gave him a quick run-down of recent events, which he greatly enjoyed, then spoke to Sandy, "What do you know about Japanese wood-block prints, Sandy? We have a prospective client who thinks some of her prints have been switched – would you be interested in following this up for us as a consultant – paid, of course? – oh good – her name is Miranda Halliwell, here is her number – you'll like her I think. We're off to the Midlands now, I'll ring you when we get back – probably late this afternoon."

Mel insisted on taking the wheel of the Riley first and they made good time to Northampton, with the statutory stop for elevenses at a truck pull-in, where they were introduced to a new delicacy – the chip butty.

"Don't let on to my Mama, Alex, she would be appalled at the harm these might do to my figure!"

"Given the way that your metabolism deals with jam tarts, my darling, I think you are in no danger!"

At the Northampton flat, they found that Stephanie was away at the station on her regular duties, but hoped to be back later. Winnie introduced them to Niels, who turned out to be rather plump, much to the surprise of Melpomene, who had been picturing a Viking type. Nevertheless, he seemed very quick, and they were soon engaged in lively exchanges of information and ideas over tea and Eccles cakes, which Mel and Alex had last enjoyed in Huddersfield. Niels said politely that they were delicious and that he would have to introduce them to Kiksekage, or biscuit cake, when they next visited him in Copenhagen, "It's made of layers of biscuits, melted chocolate and whipping cream – very rich!" he explained. Mel thought to herself, "And tends to make one plump!"

After these refreshments, talk turned to serious matters.

"Jens-Olle was delighted to hear about Mr Banfield," said Niels, "and he told me that Hugo Palance was, too. Your Scotland Yard delegate, Sir Adrian Fitz-Hugh, will interrogate him before he is charged, to extract the maximum information from him. We have already made use of what we have learnt so far – we three have noted all this in our report."

Winnie added, "You must make sure you take a copy back to London with you – I've looked through the fourth carbon, and it is quite readable. I suppose that the report will be mimeographed for wider distribution, but we haven't got the equipment for that here – we'll have to think of that as we upgrade the London office!"

"So tell me more about Luke Postlethwaite," said Melpomene, "you said he had been arrested for threatening Mildred Henderson – that would always be a hazardous act, I would judge from my short acquaintance with that lady! Did they extract anything else of value from him?"

"Only that Eliza Stanford is his aunt!" said Winnie, trying to use an off-hand tone.

"Come on, Winnie, tell us more!"

"We'll all have to wait until she has been released from hospital – her ankle was not merely sprained but broken, so it is in plaster, and they need to take more x-rays before she is considered safe to be sent home – or in this case, to the station for questioning."

The door opened at that point, and Stephanie came in, accompanied by a man in civvies and a white lab-coat. She embraced Melpomene warmly and even hugged Alex a little bit.

Before she said much more she asked, "Did you remember to bring those etchings, Mel? This is Sergeant Eric Stone, of the Northampton forensic unit, and he is anxious to check them for prints and anything else he can find."

Melpomene produced the very same cardboard box, tied up with string, that she had been given by the junk-shop woman, and handed it to Sergeant Stone with a smile, saying, "We're all on tenterhooks to find whether Satterfield and Fido Barker have had their grubby paws all over these!"

"We shall see – Mrs Crabbe, is it? If there's anything to be found, we shall find it, you can be sure of that! If you don't need the car any more, Stephanie, I'll head back to the lab with these right away."

"Now," said Stephanie, "some more news that will please all of you, I think. My estimable colleague, Jimmy Manley, has reached the exalted rank that I myself enjoy – he is now Detective-Inspector James Brian Manley! He is too modest to disclose this, but I extracted the confession from him that he has been studying hard for it for over a year!"

"We must throw a huge party to celebrate this!" said Melpomene, "as it happens, he is about to visit my family's Woodhampton Castle Hotel, at my invitation, for a few days of family holiday, so you are all invited to foregather there in a day or two to join us in the festivities! I'll let you know the date as soon I have arranged it with my Mama, Lady Cynthia!"

"To descend from the sublime to the bizarre," said Stephanie, "Jimmy informs me that some, but not all, of those murdered in the Limehouse boarding house have now been identified, mainly through fingerprint records, because they were former guests of His Majesty's Prison Service. The woman with the knife in her back regretfully died before she could be got to hospital, and has been identified as Dierdre Atkinson, with several convictions for shop-lifting and the like, but with no known involvement in art-related activities. The knife, of course was checked for fingerprints – those of Banfield and the chauffeur were found, with Banfield's on the places on the haft suggesting he was the actual stabber."

"And were the other three not stabbed?" asked Alex.

"All shot!" answered Stephanie, "and all by the chauffeur's gun – an American Smith and Wesson revolver, the so-called 'Russian' model. And this was the gun that Banfield used to dispatch the chauffeur. I'm sorry to keep saying 'the chauffeur' but we haven't made a definite identification yet. We have the names of his victims, however – they were all members of the Atkinson family – the mother, Teresa, and her two sons, Niall and Philip. Our current assumption is that these murders were ordered by Banfield – for what reason we do not know yet – and that the chauffeur was murdered to shut his mouth."

144

Stephanie invited Mel and Alex to stay for lunch, but Mel demurred, saying, "Thanks all the same, but we'll just grab a cup of tea and then we'll head off to the Big Smoke!"

Tea and more Eccles cakes having been enjoyed, they set off, Alex driving this time. After a while, Mel said, "Perhaps we should have accepted lunch after all – I have visions of chip butties or bacon sandwiches flooding into my mind!"

"I can take a hint!" said Alex, and pulled into the next lorry stop.

When they finally walked into the office, Marjorie said, looking anxious, "Scotland Yard has called two or three times – would you please ring this number as soon as you get in!"

She dialled the number, and Alex picked up the telephone, with Mel listening in.

"Mr Crabbe? Thanks for ringing back, this is Adrian Fitz-Hugh, looking forward to meeting you at the Yard as soon as possible, if you are available and willing. Now you are back in London, I'll get a car sent for you in the next few minutes. You'll be wondering what this is all about, no doubt? All I can say over the telephone is that you are not about to be arrested! Please will each of you bring some form of identification with you. I hope to see you soon!"

After a short wait, just enough time for a cup of tea, the doorbell rang and Marjorie brought in a police driver, who greeted Mel and Alex, again reminded them about the identification and took them down to a car waiting in the street – not the usual unobtrusive police vehicle, but a Daimler limousine!

At New Scotland Yard, the driver parked by the main entrance, and took them to the front desk, saying to the attendant, "Mr and Mrs Crabbe, for the Special Unit." Then he saluted and left, while the man at the desk hit a small bell. A policewoman appeared, saying, "Come with me, please, and be sure you have your identification documents ready."

She took them to the lift and up to the fourth floor, then paused at an unmarked door and pressed a button. A man dressed in a civilian suit opened the door, and held out his hand without speaking. Mel and Alex gave him a passport and a driver's licence respectively, which he inspected, then smiled and ushered them in, saying, "Sorry about the formalities, but we have to be careful! Please come with me."

He knocked at a door and waved them in, where they were greeted by a beaming Jens-Olle, Hugo Palance, a portly gentleman in a blue suit, and a tall slim man with a neatly brushed silver moustache, wearing a police uniform with insignia that neither of them had seen before.

Jens-Olle introduced the blue-suited gentleman as 'Mijnheer Petrus Wintermans, of the Netherlands Ministry of Culture' and the policeman as 'Sir Adrian Fitz-Hugh, Deputy Commissioner of the Metropolitan Police Force', and shook hands with Mel and Alex, inviting them to take their places at a long table. Hugo kissed Mel on both cheeks and then said, shaking Alex' hand, "You must be Alex! We've spoken on the telephone, of course, but never met in person!"

Fitz-Hugh offered them tea from a setting on a side-table, which they declined, Mel saying, "Later, please! I couldn't drink a thing at the moment!" and then he said, "You will have guessed, no doubt, that you are in the sanctum sanctorum of the Special Unit, set up two or three years ago for collaborative working with our European colleagues as a counter to art-related crime, which was rising to alarming levels as our countries gradually settled down after the War. One way and another, the firm of Crabbe and Crabbe has become an essential element in this struggle, and we have invited you here today to discuss our next moves."

Jens-Olle took up the explanation, "We received by police motorcycle courier this morning a copy of your Northampton division's excellent and comprehensive report, at least, Adrian did – Hugo and I will have to wait until we return home before we have our copies in our hands, but Adrian spent a couple of hours earlier taking us through it in detail. I must say, it is an extremely thorough and valuable piece of work, and describes how your work has – if I may use an English expression – shot the Art cabal full of holes! We look forward to talking to your colleagues, all together, on a later occasion. I have already spoken with Niels Mortensen and congratulated him on his part in the endeavour!"

Hugo, smiling broadly, said, "It is not in the report, but I should tell you that your client, Mr Arthur Ralston, was the key to the demolition of a long-standing web of criminals working in my country and back and forth across La Manche. And in particular he helped us unmask the despicable *Inspecteur* Fouchard, one of a nest of vipers in the bosom of my own French police force! Once uncovered, that foolish man led us further, and we rooted out more of his vile collaborators!"

"But without doubt," said Fitz-Hugh, "the pinnacle of your achievements has been the defeat of Edwin McCauley Banfield, and the unravelling of his network, including the bulk of the Atkinson clan, who have been a long-standing irritation to us in many more ways than those to do with art objects."

"It is gratifying," said Melpomene, "to think that we made a contribution, together with our stalwart staff, Marjorie Wentworth and Winifred Morris, but I want to point out that we could not have done much without the help and support of many dedicated members of the police forces of this country. I can't mention them all here – it would take too long, and you are all busy men – but I must not omit our oldest police contact, Superintendent David Wilkinson, of the Hampshire constabulary and his staff at Woodhampton. He has not been directly involved in this case, but he put us on to Chief Superintendent Freeman, in Northampton and also Chief Inspector Saunders, of the fraud squad. And there is a whole list of others who have been active in this case, out of whom I happily recognize the newly-promoted Detective Inspector Jimmy Manley, who has been a constant tower of strength!"

"I appreciate that, Melpomene – if I may call you that!" said Adrian Fitz-Hugh, "But you need not fear that anyone will be overlooked – many are already mentioned in the Northampton report – and Detective Inspector Stephanie Walters was one of the authors!"

After a period of further discussion, the group started to break up. When Alex suggested that they might dine together, Fitz-Hugh gently refused, pointing out that it was still necessary to preserve security, "When this is all tied up and sorted out, we will certainly celebrate! The unit has funds allocated for entertainment, and I myself would like to express my thanks to all concerned in some tangible way!"

The car was summoned to take Mel and Alex to their flat.

Chapter 49

Once they had related to Caroline the non-confidential details of their trip to Northampton, and drunk another few cups of tea, Melpomene said, "There must still be one or two loose ends to tidy up, surely, Alex? I shall certainly go through the report with a fine tooth-comb! Did you want to have a read of it first? If so I'll ring Northampton while you're doing that and have a talk with Winnie. Unless Stephanie has something in mind for her, it would be nice to have her back in the office!"

"There are a couple of queries I have in mind, Mel, but for the most part we can leave all the villains to the tender mercies of the police and the courts. I suppose we shall be called as witnesses in many of the hearings. I must say I am still wondering why Banfield and his cohorts suddenly descended to such violence – and the relationship between him and the chauffeur still causes me to ponder. Stephanie suggested that Banfield might have shot the chauffeur to shut him up – but by that time there was enough evidence to send them both to the gallows several times over – so what had he to gain?"

"Although they seemed to be working very closely together I didn't see any signs of an intimate liaison between the two – but I have been wrong with this sort of thing before now!" said Mel, "Maybe we shall never know! I'll phone the office first, Marjorie should still be there."

She was, but all she had to report was, "Sandy Mainwaring would like you to telephone her at your convenience to talk about her work with the Japanese prints lady. Not very urgent, tomorrow will do. If you go to Northampton to pick up Winnie, can I come too, please, Mel? It would be nice to meet Stephanie – and Niels, as well, if he's still there. We can leave Alex to mind the telephones!"

Mel said, "Certainly you can come to Northampton – it is a nice drive and you haven't ridden in the Riley yet, have you? And I have another task for you, Marjorie. We want to throw a huge party, mainly to congratulate Jimmy on his promotion, and to thank him and all the policemen – and women – and others who have been so helpful in wrapping up this case. I will telephone Mama and see whether she is willing to welcome everybody to Woodhampton Castle and decide on a date, so she will be prepared when you talk with her. So could you work on a guest-list, please, so we can check it over between us?"

When she was telephoned, Lady Cynthia was quite enthusiastic about the party, "But it will have to be soon, because Jimmy – what a nice young man he is, and what a charming family! – has to go back to work after the weekend. How about Saturday? That might be more convenient for some people than a work-day, don't you think, my dear? I look forward to working with Marjorie on all this."

The next morning, Melpomene rang Sandy at the DuPlessis Gallery. Anatole answered, as usual, so she took a moment to bring him up to date with most aspects of the case and told him about the party, which he enthused about. Then she spoke to Sandy.

"What I wanted to tell you, Mel," she said, "is that Miranda Halliwell is now satisfied that she has not been disadvantaged by the exchange of prints and does not wish to pursue the case! You should confirm this directly with her, of course."

"That's very surprising, Sandy, how did you achieve her change of heart? I assume it was something you told her, was it?"

"Yes it was, Mel. During my Art History course, we studied the Japanese wood-block print in some depth, including the techniques the masters used to produce them. Miranda Halliwell's prints are what are known as 'urushi-e', which means, literally, 'lacquer painting'. As you probably noticed they had small details picked out with metallic highlights, and if you had examined the prints closely, you might have noticed that some features had a glossy finish, hence the term 'lacquer', while others were water-based. Oh dear, I'm letting my enthusiasm carry me along!"

"Never mind, Sandy, this is all fascinating!"

"I'll get to the important part now, Mel! What I was able to tell Miranda was that during the early eighteenth century, the hey-day of the wood-block print, the concept of copyright was unknown amongst Japanese artists. Instead, the possession of a set of wood-blocks was what was important to them, so it mattered little what became of the prints themselves. By close examination, I could verify, mainly by examining the grain of the wooden blocks, which shows up in the print, that each of the prints – Miranda's original and the substitute – was pulled from the same set of blocks, and consequently both were of identical value."

"What puzzles me," said Mel, "is why, then, was the substitution made at all?"

"What I believe, and told Miranda, is that it was because of a purely sentimental attachment. She immediately sympathized with this and said that, in that case, she would not interfere, whether or not she found out who the owner was, as she herself unfailingly followed her own sentimental tendencies!"

Mel was very grateful, and told Sandy so, "I will drive over to see Miranda Halliwell myself – I'll call first to make sure she is not out riding!"

She related Sandy's story to Alex, who was very pleased, "I could do with a bit of a break in detecting right now – as long as it is not too protracted! I'm about ready to play some golf again – I know you think it is a good walk ruined – so I thought I might give Podger Ransome a call – he lives near Enfield and he's a member there – we used to play most weeks when we were students, and I've had a couple of rounds with him since."

Mel giggled. "Podger! You men and your nicknames – what is his name really? Arbuthnot? Montmorency? Clerihew?"

Alex pretended to be miffed, "Just because your parents bestowed you with a mellifluous name, you think you can put on a superior air about my friends! His name is simply Roger – I can't remember why we started to call him Podger – he is a bit tubby, I suppose!"

"By all means feel free, Alex, as long as you don't take the car when I need to go to Northampton – and bear in mind, the big party is on next weekend!"

At Miranda's house, she assured Mel that she was quite resolved not to persist with the case, but that she would nevertheless send Crabbe and Crabbe a cheque for the agreed fee.

"Please send it instead to Dr Alexandra Mainwaring, at the DuPlessis Gallery, High Street, Kensington. She did all the work and deserves the fee!"

"I'm happy to do that, Melpomene, and thanks for all you did!"

Chapter 50

On Saturday morning, the entire staff of Crabbe and Crabbe set off for Woodhampton Castle Hotel in the Riley, in a merry mood, occasionally even breaking into song. They had with them all their suitcases, including Melpomene's Louis Vuitton that had been a wedding present from her Aunt Isabel, as well as more modest items, ranging down to Alex's battered trunk from his boarding-school days, which had to be strapped on a carrier as it was too big for the boot.

The trip was enlivened by a succession of Gilbert and Sullivan duets rendered charmingly by Marjorie and Winnie, who had between them memorized most of the lyrics.

At the hotel, they were greeted by Melpomene's Mama, who kissed and hugged the two secretaries, saying, "We've heard so much about you – you know that Mel and Alex think the world of you both!"

Over lunch the two girls were introduced to Stephen and Eugenie Buckmaster and their daughter Phoebe, the Wilkinsons, and Norman and Melinda Felton, whose pregnancy was by now quite apparent. The meal was comprised mainly of cold dishes and salads, Lady Cynthia explaining that the kitchen staff were concentrating on preparations for the banquet.

Melpomene asked her Mama, "But where are Jimmy and his family? I expected to see them here – after all, they are the guests of honour! And I haven't met Mrs Manley or their children."

Lady Cynthia laughed, "I sent them off for a visit to the seaside – of course it is too late in the season for swimming or even paddling, but the children have not visited the beach very often, so they took their buckets and spades and told me they were going to build the 'biggest sandcastle in the world'! They should be back in time for afternoon tea – the children are only four and six, so they won't be coming to dinner this evening. Jimmy's wife, Mavis, is a lovely girl, and they both look after little Brian and Jennifer very well. You will see!"

The banquet, as expected, was a great success, and as Melpomene remarked to Alex, "What a pity that Hugo, Jens-

Olle and Adrian Fitz-Hugh couldn't risk it – they will have to come on a later occasion, when everything has settled down."

At the end, there were speeches, including one by a slightly embarrassed Jimmy Manley, who "Didn't know what all the fuss was about!" Melpomene proceeded to enlighten him, to roars of approbation from everyone as she mentioned each of his achievements!

After the meal, the guests all drifted into the sitting rooms or the garden room, where little knots formed and reformed, as questions were asked, experiences related and friendships blossomed.

The children, Phoebe Buckmaster's little brother Marcus and Brian and Jennifer Manley found themselves a corner and were soon playing party games involving a lot of chortling. Phoebe supervised them for a while, and then came to search out Melpomene, saying, "I hope you won't mind listening to a problem I have, but you are not in Woodhampton very often so I thought I would seize this opportunity. I think some detective work might be needed!"

Mel drew her aside to a quiet part of the room, and said, "I hope this is nothing too serious, Phoebe – have you talked about it with your father and mother?"

"Only in general terms, Mel, I am still unsure whether this is important or not. I'll tell you what happened. You may remember my school-friend Janice – you picked us up and took us home when we missed the bus that time."

"Oh, yes!" said Melpomene, "You seemed to be a very close pair!"

"Yes we are, very close, up to a week or so ago, when I found Janice crying in the lavatories at school one lunch-time. I asked her what was wrong, but she wouldn't say and got quite agitated, so I left it. Later on, after lessons has finished for the day, I asked her what was wrong again. She wasn't crying any more, but her eyes were red – but she just shook her head and turned away."

"Perhaps it was boy-friend trouble, Phoebe, you are at the age when such matters tend to crop up, aren't you?"

"I suppose so, Mel, but we are at a girls' boarding school, and so we have no chance of meeting boys during term-time, and it was a long time since the holidays. Besides, we have always shared that sort of thing when it cropped up, it has never been all that serious. I got leave to come home for this weekend, as it was special, but as far as I know, Janice is still at school. We are not allowed to have telephone calls except from our parents."

"You said this started a week ago, Phoebe. Was she still upset when you left to come here, or had things settled down by then?"

"Not very much, Mel. When Daddy came to pick me up, Janice walked with me to the car, and she appeared to be about to say something to Daddy – she has known him for ages, and they get on well – but then she seemed to change her mind, gave me a hug and a kiss, and ran back into the school – I think she was crying again."

"Where are her parents, Phoebe, can she telephone them, did she say anything about that?"

"That is a bit of a problem, too, Melpomene. Her father is some sort of diplomat, and so she hardly ever sees him or her mother – they are always off in some other country. She comes to stay with me sometimes in the holidays, and once in a while goes to stay with them wherever they are posted at the time. She has an auntie, too, but she lives in Scotland. As far as I know she has stayed with her only once or twice."

"Well, Phoebe, would you like me to look into this a bit? I can't promise any results, but if we don't try we won't get anywhere. Write down for me the name of your school and of the headmistress, and Janice's name and the names of her parents, and anything else you think of – write down as much detail as you can and give it to me. Alex and I will be here at the hotel until late tomorrow, and you know our office and home telephone numbers, I think. Will you leave us to do what we can?"

"Oh, yes, Melpomene – that has made me feel a lot better already!" and Phoebe gave her a kiss and a big hug, then ran off.

Mel found Alex and said, "We may have just picked up another case, although it might not amount to anything. We shall see!"

FIN

KEEP VIGILANT FOR THE NEXT CASE!

Crabbe and Crabbe's next case will be coming out soon!

Will there be murders? Who knows.

Will there be skullduggery? Undoubtedly.

Will Melpomene and Alex solve the case?

Of course – how could anyone doubt this!

Look out for:

"The Problem with Janice"

A Case for Crabbe and Crabbe.

By Geoffrey Foster

Coming in a few months.

www.ingramcontent.com/pod-product-compliance
Lightning Source LLC
Chambersburg PA
CBHW052142170626
46812CB00004B/1559